IRREVOCABLE RESOLUTION

**Alan Joubert Series
Book #2**

Al Dugan

What critics had to say about the Alan Joubert Series Book #1,
Absolute Resolution

"Drama, romance, and action can be found inside this well-written tale. Overall, I highly recommend this brilliant military novel to readers everywhere."

—*Manhattan Book Review*

"Author Al Dugan has written an action-packed thriller that will keep readers turning the pages for the next exciting scene. And they come quickly, one after another."

—*San Francisco Book Review*

This is a work of fiction. Names, characters, businesses, places, events, and incidents are either products of the author's imagination or used in a fictitious manner. Any resemblance to actual persons, living and dead, or actual events is purely coincidental.

ISBN: 1535318414
ISBN 13: 9781535318419
Library of Congress Control Number: 2016916040
CreateSpace Independent Publishing Platform
North Charleston, South Carolina

Special thanks to Aaron Dugan Morrill, my grandson, for the design of the cover.

CHAPTER 1

PUPPY IN VENEZUELA: 1982

The large windows of his top-floor, corner office in the Ochoa building in Old San Juan, Puerto Rico, provided an excellent view of the harbor below. Only the channel into the harbor was blocked by El Morro, the Spanish fort, which had been built to guard the harbor entrance. It was Monday morning, and Fortune' Alan Joubert was at his desk at 7:30 a.m., as usual. As a mariner, he was enjoying the view. A Sealand container ship was approaching the dock, assisted by two tugs. Directly across the harbor, an Integrated Tug Barge was maneuvering to dock at the rice co-op with its easily visible large white cylindrical silos for rice storage. It was a typical beautiful sunny start to the day. This marine activity boded well for his deep-cover job as an expatriate marine consultant for Sea Secure, a large US marine insurance company out of New York. He was waiting for the call he knew was coming shortly.

The telephone rang on time, and he picked up on the first ring. He knew it was his CIA handler for a new covert assignment for the Absolute Resolution program. Joubert had been sheep dipped into the CIA for the Operation Phoenix in Vietnam after one and a half tours as a decorated marine recon captain. The current CIA Absolute Resolution project was engaged in espionage and assassination work in the Caribbean and throughout Central and South America.

"Alan here," he answered; he preferred his middle name.

"Good morning, Alan," Robert Johnson responded. "We have a pure reconnaissance intelligence mission for you down in Venezuela. You have a package that will be delivered shortly. We have intelligence that arms are being shipped into Puerto Cabello for the FARC communist insurgents in Colombia. It appears the Colombians have finally stopped the inflow of weapons through their ports. The Russians and Cubans are now apparently shipping the weapons through Venezuela and smuggling them across the border."

"Why isn't this matter being handled internally by the Venezuelan customs or security forces?"

"Well, because some of the good guys in customs and security are part of the smuggling rings. They're in it only for the money; we understand the payoff is a significant amount per shipment. There's a large shipment scheduled to arrive in a week. We do not want to intercept the shipment before Venezuela and give away the fact we're tracking the whole project back to the sources, but we do want to stop this shipment. We have one trusted security guy at the port who can help you when you get there. He doesn't want to do anything but let you know exactly where you can find the shipment stored in the port before it's picked up. He knows if the smugglers catch him, he will disappear, along with his family. We want you to attach a tracking device to each of the cargo crates so we can track the shipments. As soon as they cross into Colombia, we will work with the Colombians to destroy the weapons with air strikes."

"Well," Alan replied tapping his pen on his desk, "it sure seems like the Venezuelan security guy, if he was careful, could take care of it. I expect you're setting up a cover for me to get in the port facility?"

"A shell CIA company will be making a shipment to correspond with the timing of this shipment. The shipment will be damaged and insured by Sea Secure, and you will be there to inspect the damages. The shell company will contact the port authorities and freight forwarder to let them know you are coming to inspect their cargo for an insurance claim."

"Roger that; I'll call if I have any questions once I review the mission package" Alan said before hanging up.

The package came at 8:30 a.m. marked URGENT—PERSONAL & CONFIDENTIAL. Ana, his secretary, delivered it back to his office and closed the door on her way out. Alan reviewed the file documents, all on burn paper. Also included in the package were six small tracking devices and brief operating instructions. Given the size, the battery life was only five days; they were only to be turned on at the time they were attached to the cargo. Alan would be given at least twenty-four hours' notice before departure on the mission.

The rest of the week was quiet, both at Sea Secure and the CIA. Alan continued his everyday routine of working 7:30 a.m. to 5:00 p.m. in his office and then going home and taking a two-mile run in Luchetti Park. This was followed by an hour and a half of body-surfing on the beach in front of his condo in Condado.

Alan's pager went off Saturday afternoon. Alan called back, and Robert picked up on the first ring.

"We have a go on Venezuela," Robert said. "We need you to fly out Sunday afternoon. Your inspection has been set up for late Monday afternoon. We'll have a ticket waiting at the airport in San Juan.

"Hold on, let me get a pen and paper," Alan said as he reached for his pen and note pad.

"You'll be on Eastern Airlines Flight 92 connecting through Miami. You'll also have a flight booked on Conviasa Airlines Monday morning to Puerto Cabello and a National rental car reserved when you arrive. You'll be staying at the Hilton in Caracas Sunday night, and there will be no field support provided. You will treat the trip as any other Sea Secure assignment."

"Roger that," Alan acknowledged before signing off.

Alan caught the flight and arrived in Caracas late Sunday night. He spent the night at the Hilton. Alan had a glass of wine and a steak dinner before it turned in.

Monday morning Alan left the hotel by cab at 7:00 a.m. for his 8:00 a.m. flight to Puerto Cabello. The flight would be a quick forty-five minutes—about a hundred miles from Caracas. Puerto Cabello is the largest port in Venezuela. *Cabello* in Spanish is a hair; the port was so called because the water was so calm you could tie up a ship with a single hair.

The cab driver got on the main expressway, and it was jammed bumper to bumper for as far as they could see ahead.

"I have to make this flight. Are there any other options?" Alan said after assessing the traffic nightmare.

"Piece of cake," the cab driver responded. He pulled to the shoulder of the road and began backing down the freeway. He backed for about a half mile until he reached an on-ramp, and then he began backing down the ramp on the shoulder, with cars blasting their horns at them. Within ten minutes the cab pulled up in front of the departure terminal at the Conviasa Airlines door at the National Airport.

The cab driver turned and said, "Piece of cake," one more time, pointing at the terminal door. Alan could not stop laughing as he paid the driver and added a twenty-dollar tip. All Alan could think about was Fast Eddie, the sniper on his marine recon team in Vietnam, who was famous for using the phrase "piece of cake" in the most dangerous situations.

The flight to Puerto Cabello was short and uneventful. Alan picked up his car at National Rental Car and headed to the port. He planned to stop and eat lunch, as his meeting at the port to review the damaged CIA plant cargo was set for 2:00 p.m. When the opportunity looked right, he would page the security contact at the port so he could be directed to the arms shipment that was to be tagged with the electronic trackers.

Alan showed up at the main security gate at 1:45 p.m. and provided the name of the freight forwarder who was the contact for the damaged cargo insured by Sea Secure. The manager of the freight forwarder came to the gate, and Alan was issued a visitor's security badge, as well as a pass for his car. Alan followed the freight forwarder manager to warehouse six for the inspection.

The CIA-shipped equipment, part of an assembly-line conveyor system, had purposefully been improperly crated, and thus the expected damage had occurred. Alan hired some longshoremen to remove the equipment from the two crates so he could carefully inspect and photograph it. After it was unloaded, everyone left Alan alone. The freight manager gave Alan his pager number and advised Alan to turn in his security badge and car pass at the main gate when he left.

Alan immediately walked over to the pay telephone at the warehouse doorway and called his security contact at the port facility pager to direct him to the arms shipment. The security man, Juan, called back within minutes.

"Red," Alan answered.

"Black," Juan quickly responded with the security-code response.

"I'm at warehouse six. I'm free and ready to go."

"OK. The cargo, five crates, is in warehouse two. You need to walk out the main door of warehouse six and turn right. Warehouse two is a hundred fifty meters down. The crates are on the left wall near the rear corner of the warehouse when you enter the main door. I just completed a check of some other nearby cargo, and there are two men guarding the crates. At least one of the men had a gun. When I came around the corner, he pulled the gun out of his jacket and questioned me. I showed him my supervisor badge, and he put the gun away. He and his partner had visitor's passes. They advised me they were hired private guards. In my twenty years, I have not seen this type of security for a shipment."

"Thanks. I don't need anything else."

"OK. Be careful. The men look very dangerous."

Alan placed his camera and notepad next to his briefcase. He opened the false-bottom compartment of his briefcase and pulled out his combat knife. This was going to be interesting—going to a gunfight with a knife. He packed his camera and notepad in the briefcase and zipped his jacket halfway. The combat knife, with the clasp loose, was on his waistband under the Windbreaker.

Alan made sure his visitor's security badge was clearly visible at the top of his half-zipped jacket. He started down to warehouse two.

Alan entered the warehouse and walked down the middle aisle of the stacked cargo, looking completely lost. He reached the back wall, turned left, and headed toward the area where the arms-shipment crates were stored. When he got to the edge of the last aisle, he could see the two men guarding the crates. One man was sitting in a folding chair reading a newspaper, and the other was clearly on watch.

Alan turned the corner, still looking lost. He was five feet away from the man standing on watch and eight feet away from the man sitting in the chair. The man on watch immediately pulled his gun, a .45-caliber Colt, and quietly said, "Don't move. Why are you here?"

Alan spoke in as poor a Spanish accent as he could. "Yo soy un perrito. Yo estoy para la inspección de carga." ("I am a puppy. I am here for a cargo inspection.") He continued to move forward and stared at the racked cargo.

Both men immediately started laughing, and the man who had been reading the newspaper immediately lost interest and went back to reading. The other man lowered his gun and with a big smile said, "Eres un perito. No eres un perrito, idiota." ("You are a marine surveyor. You are not a puppy, idiot.") He had another big laugh.

Alan had closed within a few feet, and at that very moment, he quickly lunged and thrust his left fist into the gunman's throat. The gunman immediately collapsed to his knees, dropped his gun, and fell on the ground face first. His windpipe crushed, he gasped for air. The man in the chair, caught completely off guard, hesitated just long enough for Alan to lunge and give him a full-leg kick to the head as he tried to jump out of the chair. The man crashed backward, and Alan closed and caught him in a headlock chokehold. He held the struggling man until he passed out. Then Alan quickly and violently twisted his head, breaking his neck.

Alan checked the gunman's pulse, and he was dead as well. Alan had noticed some empty crates on the back wall of the warehouse that had been opened, and their crate tops were leaning against the wall. Alan picked up each man, military-buddy style, and dropped him in the empty crate along with the gun. He then placed the top on the crate so it appeared it was loaded with cargo.

Alan pulled five of the six trackers from the false-bottom compartment on his briefcase. He photographed the shipping labels, as well as each crate. He carefully examined under the skids on the crates to figure out where he could affix the trackers so they would not be damaged by forklifts. The trackers had two one-inch nails, and Alan had a small ball peen hammer. He turned each tracker switch on and attached one to each crate. Alan used his ball peen hammer to drive the partially pulled nails into the top panel of the crate that held the two dead men.

Alan returned to warehouse six to pick up his car. He did not have to do any more work on the cargo shipped by the CIA; the CIA shell company would just have the freight forwarder recrate it and ship it back. Alan got in his rental car and drove to the main gate, returning both his security visitor pass and the car pass. He drove to the airport to return the rental car. He had time to call Robert collect from a pay telephone, as his flight was late.

Robert answered on the second ring.

"The crates are all tagged. I'm heading back to Caracas in thirty minutes. I'll be flying to Puerto Rico, by way of Miami, tomorrow morning. Can you have logistics book my return flight?"

"Roger that. We have an aircraft on a training mission with the Venezuelans, and they have already picked up the trackers on the crates in Puerto Cabello. Well done."

"I had to take out a couple of armed bad guys that were guarding the crates. I dumped them in an empty crate on the back wall twenty feet from the crates with the trackers. I nailed it shut. Hopefully no one will find them before the arms-shipment crates leave."

"Roger that. Was there any blood?"

"No blood. Nice and clean."

"Excellent. Call me when you get back to PR," Robert said before signing off.

The flight back from Puerto Cabello to Caracas left forty-five minutes late in a pouring rainstorm. Alan hated small commuter planes, especially these de Havilland Dash 8 turboprops, where the gate personnel even weighed your briefcase to assure proper weight distribution and limits.

The next morning it was really a relief to board an Eastern Airlines jet for the trip back to Puerto Rico. It was a Bloody-Mary morning. Alan had not expected wet work and still needed to wind down.

CHAPTER 2

BACK IN PUERTO RICO

Alan was back at his desk the next morning at the usual time and had closed the door. His first call was to Robert to provide the details of the completed mission.

"How did you take those two guys so cleanly?" Robert asked.

"Hand to hand, but as usual I had the element of complete surprise. It was all over in a minute."

"Impressive. The legend continues. We had the crate with the dead guards picked up, and they've been disposed of, so the operation is 100% clean. Both the guys had guns; one man's gun was still in his shoulder holster. You sure did a great job of improvising—and you didn't spill a drop of blood. We didn't even have to call the cleaners before the cargo was picked up. Great job," Robert said and then signed off.

Ana, always well dressed with her dark hair pinned up, knocked on Alan's office door shortly after he hung up.

"Good morning, boss. How was your trip to Venezuela?"

"Everything went smoothly. The cargo is being shipped back to the manufacturer. The shipment was not properly packed, so the shipper has withdrawn the claim, and I won't need to send a report—just a telex."

The rest of the week was quiet at Sea Secure. Alan did take off Friday afternoon, *viernes social,* as was the custom of executives in Puerto Rico. He went home early, took a two-mile run, and body-surfed for two hours. He would stay home this weekend, read, listen to jazz, and work out.

Sunday Alan got in an hour and a half of bodysurfing and returned to the rented beach chair under an umbrella in front of his condo on Condado Beach. He dried off, sat, and took a sip of his Corona beer. It was a bright and sunny afternoon. The views of the aquamarine and dark-blue waters and the trade winds blowing through the palm trees on the beach were deeply relaxing and calming.

Alan was still grieving for Maria, the local NCIS agent with whom he had fallen deeply in love; she had been ambushed six months ago and killed by the *Independentistas* known as *Los Macheteros.* These same terrorists had attacked a navy commuter bus in a vicious ambush, killing two sailors and wounding ten. Alan had more than settled the score, but the deep longing for Maria, who had become his soul mate, would take a long time to heal. He missed Maria the most on Sundays, which they used to spend on the beach together.

Alan, working rogue and off the grid, had eliminated the five shooters who had ambushed and killed Maria and her partner and attacked the navy bus. Rene Dubois, ex-SEAL and Alan's partner in Vietnam on Operation Phoenix, had helped him. Alan and Rene had passed lie-detector tests after the fact, as they had several times in 'Nam when they knew they were doing the right thing. Although Alan's CIA handler had known that the deaths were the work of Alan and Rene, he'd quickly moved on. Alan had been far too successful and productive in the Absolution Resolution wetwork assignments to lose. Elimination of the terrorists had been the goal, and now the threat to US military personnel in Puerto Rico had been eliminated.

Alan had made sure he had taken Sonia, an NCIS officer who had been a close friend of Maria, aside to give her all the other information he had uncovered on the logistics operation of the Independentistas. Sonia was assigned to the investigation on the remaining Independentistas' logistics support personnel and donors.

Monday Alan was at his desk at the usual time and closed his door. He would be letting Sea Secure know he would be extending his expatriate contract for another two years. George, the CEO at Sea Secure, had offered to increase his salary by 35 percent and increase the benefits offered under the expatriate program. Alan would also let the CIA know he would be extending his contract for the Absolute Resolution program for two years. The CIA had agreed to a 15 percent increase in his salary, based on his additional two-year contract in Puerto Rico.

He called George, the CEO of Sea Secure, first.

George's assistant answered and asked Alan to hold. Within minutes, George's booming voice was on the line. "Alan, I'm so glad to hear from you. I knew you'd get back to me in thirty days as promised, and it's been almost exactly thirty days."

"I'm doing fine, boss. I've really been taking it easy and spending a lot of time on the beach, trying to get back to a normal life. I've decided I'll accept your generous offer for another two year contract, as well as your ex-roomie's offer for my CIA work. I really appreciate it. I am honored."

"Excellent," George said, a distinct note of pleasure in his gravelly voice. "I couldn't be happier. I can assure you all the staff and our customers in Puerto Rico, the Caribbean, Central America, and South America will also be happy. The human resources folks will be sending you the official package. I've also signed off on the increased expatriate expense items we discussed. Thank you so much for taking this important issue off my plate. I'm glad to have it resolved."

"Great. I look forward to continue working here for Sea Secure. I wasn't sure I could stay on in Puerto Rico after Maria, but I've found I actually feel closer to her to be here. I'll be going to dinner at her parents' house next weekend," Alan said as he shifted in his chair and took a deep breath, "I expect this will help them as well. My next call is to your ex-roomie at the CIA, and I'll say hello."

"Great. Say hello and tell my ex-roomie he owes me a round of golf, drinks, and dinner."

"Will do. Thanks. See you in New York in two months."

"See you then," George said and signed off.

Alan next dialed Robert Johnson, his CIA handler for the Absolute Resolution program.

Robert picked up the operations line after several rings. "Robert here."

"I've decided to sign up for another two years in Puerto Rico with Sea Secure and Absolute Resolution."

"Well, everyone, including the top man, is going to be very happy about this. I'm so glad you've decided to stay on. We don't have anyone better than you," Robert stated sincerely. "The promised fifteen percent raise will be effective today. I have some more assignments in the pipeline; they should start up in a few weeks."

"I'm ready. Let me know."

***

On Sunday Alan arrived at 5:30 p.m. for dinner with Maria's parents. Marta looked beautiful and elegant as always. Federico looked worn and it was obvious he was not sleeping well. Alan brought filet mignon to barbeque and a bottle of Chianti Classico. Maria's father grilled the steaks perfectly, medium rare, and Marta made an excellent Caesar salad and black beans. They talked almost the entire time about Maria; remembering the good times was helping all of them to move forward.

When Alan got up to say good night and leave, he walked over and gave Maria's mom a kiss on the check. She stood and hugged Alan.

"I want to let you know I have extended my expatriate contract with Sea Secure for another two years. At first I thought staying in Puerto Rico would be difficult."

"We're so happy," Marta said as she hugged Alan again.

"Alan, you'll always be family, and we hope you'll come again for a Sunday dinner. You're welcome any time," Federico, a retired marine sergeant major, said as he gave Alan a quick hug and a firm handshake.

"That sounds like a deal, but no saluting," Alan said with a smile.

Alan had also set up a dinner with Sonia on Friday.

Sonia and Alan met for an early dinner at Metropol in Ocean Beach. Alan was waiting for Sonia when she arrived. She looked beautiful as always, but still had a visible sadness in her dark brown eyes after losing her best friend Maria. They gave each other a hug and kiss on the cheeks, and then they were led to Alan's favorite table.

"How's it going, Sonia?"

"I'm getting better. I still have vivid dreams of Maria, but they are all the good times. Still miss her every moment. How are you?"

"I'm better," Alan said in a heavy voice blinking back a tear. "I only wish Maria and I could have at least had more time, but I cherish every moment we had together. I think every day of all the things I never had time to tell her or do with her."

"She loved you so deeply, and I know it was a two-way street," Sonia said. She gazed out the window at people walking to the restaurant and bit her lip and cleared her throat, "I wanted you to know we have arrested and charged all the logistics personnel and donors for the Independentistas that you provided to us. John Marshall, the supervising agent, was very suspicious that we wrapped it up so quickly after all the accidents and mishaps with the shooters, but the results make him look good. He called me in to let me know he had no doubt where all the intel had come from and that you'd better not ever cross NCIS again."

"Yes, I heard he was still really pissed off. Well, so goes it."

Alan and Sonia finished up with Cuban expressos. They hugged and kissed cheeks, before saying good-bye. His heart ached for Maria and her sparkling eyes and joyous laugh.

CHAPTER 3

VIVA LA DEMOCRACIA

Alan was at his desk Monday morning when a courier delivered a package, which Ana brought back to his office. The package was an assignment from a shipping company in Canada requesting a quote for an entire pressboard factory in Arecibo, Puerto Rico, to be shipped and then unloaded in Mazatlán, Mexico, in the state of Sinaloa. The ship that would be used was a ten-thousand-ton Greek tramper with five hold tweendecker. Alan would have to drive to Arecibo to do a walk-around in the factory to determine the scope and quote for the consulting services. He made a call to the marine superintendent of the shipping company and advised him he'd arrive in Arecibo on Thursday.

Alan called Robert on the contact number, and Robert picked up on the second ring.

"Good morning, Alan. It has been quiet around here. FYI, the trackers worked perfectly. The Colombians hit the truck with an air strike when the truck was twenty-five klicks inside Colombia."

"Excellent. I called you to let you know I am going to be quoting a large marine-consulting project for Sea Secure. I'll have to review all the packing plans, as well as complete the stowage plan for the ship. After that I can have one of my guys attend the packing and loading in case you need me. I'll be out of pocket for about two weeks unless you have a code-red emergency."

"Roger that, Robert replied "Does the job include supervising unloading in Mazatlán?"

"Yes, but I can have one of my team handle the discharge. That won't be a problem."

"We may have an assignment in Sinaloa near Mazatlán. The top man just mentioned it to me about an hour ago. Let me get some more information and the time constraints, and I'll get back to you. When do you think the unloading in Mazatlán will occur?"

"Probably in about forty-five days, if everything stays on schedule."

"OK. I'll get back to you once I get more information. If there's no time constraint, this could be a great reason for you to be in Mazatlán. I also wanted to let you know an alert was sent out to all port personnel in Puerto Cabello asking if they had seen or had any information on the whereabouts of the two missing private security guards. Our trusted security guy has also advised us the port has pulled the list of all visitors and employees in the port on the day you were there, as well as the day after. We should have the list shortly; he's getting us a copy, so we can review the number of people in and out of the port on those two days. Given your strong cover for being on site, I don't think it'll be a problem."

"Roger that. Talk soon." Alan signed off.

Ana knocked on his door when she saw he was off the line.

"We have a fire you need to handle. You've got a really pissed-off broker. You may have to get over to him today. One of the underwriters decided not to provide coverage for a large risk he presented and apparently let it sit on his desk for close to a week before making the decision."

"I'll handle it. Looks like we have an opportunity for a big assignment for a factory shipment. Tell Miguel I'll need him to come with me to Arecibo on Thursday to review the project."

"Will do," Ana said. She walked out and closed the door.

Alan and Miguel visited the pressboard factory on Thursday. They inspected the many long rows of linked conveyor rollers that press the husks of sugar cane into pressboard for use in construction. Alan submitted a quote for a daily rate and necessary expenses. Sea Secure was awarded the contract, and Alan reviewed the packing plan and made corrections and adjustments. The ship began loading a week later.

It took a week to load the ship and secure the cargo. The ship's crew members were all Greeks, and the captain was an old-time professional. Unlike American flagships, the Greeks served alcohol with dinner each night. To save time, Alan and Miguel ate their meals on the ship and got to know all the crew.

The ship sailed on schedule, and they planned to arrive using the Panama Canal in three weeks. The day the ship sailed, Alan called Robert to update him on the project.

"I just wanted to let you know the ship is underway with an ETA of approximately three weeks. I'll have three days' notice before the ship arrives for discharge in Mazatlán. If you don't need me, I'll send my team member."

"Thanks for the update. I should be able to discuss the potential assignment with you by the end of the week. You may not like it."

"That's not encouraging. I was certainly wondering what work might be in Mexico."

"Talk more soon," Robert said and signed off.

The rest of the week was quiet. Sonia had called to invite Alan to a party on Saturday, but he just did not feel like a party yet. He knew he would have to get a social life soon, but right now, it just did not feel right. It was soon to go to a party, especially with a group that had been friends with Maria.

Robert called two days later. "Alan, is your door closed?"

"Yes. We can talk."

"Well, let me lay this assignment out, and all I ask is you let me finish completely before you make a decision."

"That sounds ominous."

"The CIA director was contacted by the director of the DEA. Two DEA agents were abducted, tortured, beheaded, and then put on display in Sinaloa near Mazatlán. It was definitely the local drug cartel, and the director of the DEA is looking for a way to show these guys what will happen if they do this again. I know what you'll say right away: Why not send in the SEALs? This of course was everyone's first option. But the State Department required approval from the Mexican government at the highest levels, and the request was denied. The Mexican government officials said they would handle it. Of course they haven't, which we know because we've maintained twenty-four-hour satellite surveillance of El Jefe's house since our request. That tells you the level of importance. The Mexicans don't know about the surveillance. The top gun at the Directorate of Operations wants you to go after El Jefe."

Alan leaned back in his chair and crossed his arms, "This doesn't sound like an Absolute Resolution assignment."

"I knew this would be your first response. Honestly I think they have run out of other options. As you would guess, he is heavily guarded and has top-notch security at his house; wet work outside the house would probably be the best opportunity. I have a full package with a great deal of intel that was sent today and will be delivered to you tomorrow. Timing is not critical, as El Jefe rarely leaves the area. The director of the DEA does not care when—just that it is done."

Alan sat quietly for several minutes. Robert was used to this. Finally Alan replied, "Send me the package, and I'll see what I think might work. No promises on this one. Can't we accidentally drop a BLU-82 Daisy Cutter on the compound?"

"I wish. Read over what I have sent. I haven't promised the top guy anything; I cautioned him that this is not really an appropriate use of a critical and valuable asset in the Absolute Resolution program. That certainly gave him pause and asked me to send the package to you and get your feedback."

The next day Alan received the package. Ana brought the package marked URGENT—PERSONAL & CONFIDENTIAL back to Alan and then closed his door on her way out.

The package was very large. Alan opened the package and quickly examined the extensive collection of documents, maps, and photos, which were all marked Top Secret. This was going to take a while.

Alan called Robert, who picked up on the second ring. "I got the package and did a quick review. Given the volume of intel, I'll need this week and weekend to complete the review. I'm sure I can get back to you no later than next Monday morning."

"Roger that. Not surprised at all. I look forward to hearing from you when you finish your review. I'm concerned about using you for this assignment. If you review everything and don't feel it's a go for you, I'll back you one hundred percent. Call me when you are ready to discuss. I'll give the boss an update on your review schedule."

They signed off, and Alan put the large package of intel into his briefcase. He would start his review at home that night, working each night into the weekend.

Alan finished his review of the file on El Jefe late Saturday night. He spent all day at the beach on Sunday relaxing and body-surfing. Several women flirted with him, and he just nodded and politely smiled. Alan just was not ready for any kind of a relationship after Maria.

Monday Alan was at his desk early as usual, and he closed his door and called Robert.

"I am glad you really took your time on this one," Robert said when he answered.

"Well, I struggled with this one. I think it is going to be really dangerous. I think the deciding factor for me was the family information on the DEA agents who were tortured and murdered. I need to discuss ground rules. I would expect El Jefe has a list of enemies, including other cartels, so no restrictions on how I get this done?"

"I have already discussed this aspect with the top guy, and he spoke to the director of the DEA. They don't care how you do it, but don't get caught. I thought you would enjoy that one."

"Right," Alan chuckled. "I got that one. OK, I'll handle it. I'll send you a list of what I need in country. You will have to have a local company guy deliver it to me when I am ready. I'll call you when I get notice to leave for Mazatlán to discharge the ship. The only person I want to know I'm in-country is the Mexico City CIA operations guy who will deliver my required package. No one else is to know. This one is just too dangerous to have any chance of a security leak by the Mexicans."

"Roger that," Robert said. "I fully understand. I'll let the top guy know. If this was anyone else but you, I would have turned down the assignment and just sent back the intel."

Alan sent a courier package to Robert with what he needed delivered to him in Mazatlán. Three days later Alan received the notice for the ship arrival schedule, so he flew out to Mexico City and connected to Mazatlán. He was staying at the same hotel as Ivan, the marine superintendent of the shipping company.

The ship arrived on schedule, and when the hatches were opened, the cargo was all in perfect condition. It took five days to fully discharge the ship. On the final day, the governor of the state of Sinaloa, who had purchased the pressboard factory, was scheduled for a dinner on board the ship, sponsored by the shipping company. The dinner was fun and loud, and everyone consumed a great deal of cocktails and wine. Even the governor's two bodyguards were drinking. At the end of the dinner, toasts were offered. The Greek captain broke out a bottle of ouzo and passed around shots. After another hour, things were getting very loud.

Alan and Ivan had to pull the Greek chief engineer off the governor when he hugged him and screamed, "Viva la democracia!"

Ivan announced the dinner was over. The governor immediately responded, "I want you, Alan, and the captain to come out to my favorite club and have a drink with me before we call it quits."

Alan tried to signal no to Ivan, but it was too late. "Sure. We would be honored to have a drink with you."

The group, including the two bodyguards, headed for the gangway. The ship was now fully unloaded, so the long articulating gangway was very steep. The governor was the first to the gangway. He took the first step and fell, tumbling down. All the rest of the party stared in horror as the governor rolled all the way to the bottom of the long aluminum gangway, where he jumped up and shouted, "Come on! Let's go!"

Apparently God does watch over fools and drunkards. Alan smiled as they all started carefully down.

Ivan, the marine superintendent, grabbed Alan by the arm at the bottom of the gangway. "One drink, and then we catch a cab. Thank God the governor didn't die falling down the vessel gangway."

"He is going to hurt tomorrow," Alan said with a laugh.

After one drink, Alan, Ivan, and the captain said their goodbyes. The governor gave each a business card and let them know if they ever had problems in Sinaloa, they should give him a call.

Alan sent a message to the pager of the CIA operations contact who was going to deliver the package. He confirmed he would be checking into the Sheraton at 11:00 a.m. the next day for the planned package drop-off. Alan turned in for a much-needed rest and still could not help laughing at the thought of the governor tumbling down the gangway and jumping up at the bottom, ready to rock and roll.

The next morning Alan checked out of the Holiday Inn where they had been staying and caught a cab over to the Sheraton. He had told the marine superintendent he was flying to Puerto Rico early that afternoon. Once he was in his room, he paged his room number to the ops man making the package delivery.

At exactly 11:00 a.m., Alan heard the code: three hard knocks, two light knocks, followed by one harder knock. This was code indicating, "I am here, and no bad guys are with me." Alan glanced through the door's peephole and then opened the door.

The ops guy was in his midforties, athletic, with the beginnings of silver streaks in his hair. "Bob Cranson. Glad to meet you," he said as he set a large duffel on the floor.

"Thanks. Appreciate the delivery."

"I was told to tell you we can't help you at all moving forward. I don't even know what's in the duffel. Good luck. I've got to run," he said and then walked away.

Alan opened the duffel and began examining the contents. He first pulled out two M72 66 mm Light Anti-Tank Weapons (LAWs). Next were four claymore antipersonnel mines, each with trip wires and the standard detonator wire and trigger. The duffel also had an M14 with a folding stock and two hundred rounds of ammunition, a Berretta 92S-1 pistol with fifty rounds of ammunition, a combat vest, an infrared scope, a combat knife, and camouflage greasepaint. He had everything he had requested.

The most recent intel report was also included. Every night at approximately 8:00 p.m., El Jefe left his highly fortified compound and drove into Mazatlán. He had dinner at his favorite restaurant and then went to a local strip club. He would return home around midnight. His vehicle was a custom armored SUV, purchased from a specialty manufacturer in the United States. The security vehicles, one ahead and one behind, were just ordinary GMC SUVs. Each contained two men with AK47s and pistols.

The compound was located fifteen miles out of town and was completely isolated in the foothills. It had a fifteen-foot-high wall surrounding the two-acre property. The security was on par with a typical CIA compound in a hostile area.

That afternoon Alan rented a car and drove down the road that passed El Jefe's compound. He was only carrying his Berretta. He had already reviewed detailed aerial photos, and there were no surprises. He slowed down at the location he had chosen and pulled over, pretending to check his tires. The elevation would be perfect—just as it had appeared in the aerial photos.

When he returned to the hotel, he ate dinner and returned to his room. He was running the plan through his head. At 8:00 p.m. he drove back toward the compound, pulling off the road halfway there when he reached the spot he had chosen. He parked his car behind a large rock so that it could not be seen from the road.

He applied the camouflage grease to his face, pulled on his combat vest, and loaded his gear. He carried the four claymore antipersonnel mines to the road and wired them carefully, pulling the wires back to his position. The backsides of the claymores had reflector tape so he would clearly be able to see them with the infrared scope. He put two on each side of the road, seventy-five feet apart, with their front blast zones facing the road. He ran the wiring back to the gully in front of the large rock where his car was parked and connected the trigger.

He then moved the duffel up to the gully and laid out the two M72 LAWs, the M14, and six loaded magazines. Now it was time for the hardest part: waiting.

At 11:45 p.m. Alan picked up the lights of a convoy of vehicles. He checked with his scope, and it was clearly El Jefe on the way home. There was normally no traffic in the area, especially at this time of night. When the vehicles were 200 yards away, moving at about sixty miles per hour, Alan picked up the custom license plate of the lead security SUV. He picked up an M72 LAW and flipped the safety off. The weapon was fitted with a red-dot sight. Alan waited until El Jefe's armored SUV was in the middle of the claymores, and then he aimed and fired the M72 LAW round at the front-end wheel area. The rocket roared away, hitting and destroying the lower front end of El Jefe's SUV. The driver stepped on the brakes and skidded to a stop in the middle of the two-lane highway. The two escort SUVs both slammed on their brakes; they were also stopped in the middle of the claymores.

Alan picked up the other M72 LAW and fired it at the lead SUV escort. The unarmored SUV was completely destroyed by the rocket hit. The driver of El Jefe's armored SUV tried to back up, but the front-end damage was so severe the vehicle barely moved. The tail SUV quickly pulled forward alongside El Jefe's damaged SUV to provide cover from the side of attack. Alan could see the doors of the armored SUV opening, with El Jefe and the two others in the damaged SUV trying to get into the unarmored tail SUV.

Alan ducked and triggered all four of the claymores at once. The claymore antipersonnel mines, each with its seven hundred one-eighth-inch steel balls powered by C-4 explosives, devastated the two vehicles. Alan grabbed his M14 and sprinted toward the heavily damaged vehicles. The unarmored SUV looked like Swiss cheese. El Jefe was crawling between the two vehicles, bleeding heavily. Alan saw that no one else was moving, and he walked over and planted his foot on El Jefe's back.

"This is for the two DEA agents and their families," Alan said quietly before he shot him in the back of the head. He then checked and confirmed all the others were dead.

He packed all of his gear in the duffel and drove back onto the main road to Mazatlán. Two miles down the road, he pulled over and used a towel he had brought to wipe the camouflage grease off his face. He pulled into the garage at the Sheraton and parked, and then he brought the duffel back to his room.

He paged the CIA ops contact who had delivered the duffel to let him know he could come back as planned and to retrieve it.

The contact came one hour later and picked up the duffel. Alan shook his hand, but there was no discussion.

Alan took a long shower and scrubbed himself clean of the heavy smell of cordite. His flight back to Puerto Rico, connecting in Mexico City, was scheduled for the next day at 9:30 a.m.

It was definitely time for a nightcap. The hotel bar only had a handful of other patrons. Alan had a glass of California Pinot Noir before returning to his room. He did not sleep well, and woke up several times on full alert after the intense action.

The flights back were uneventful—first class with a couple of Bloody Marys just to further wind down.

CHAPTER 4

NEW YORK: 1982

Alan called Robert from his office when he got in.
"Wow, you really hit them hard," Robert said. "The Mexicans sent us photos and video. I just saw the list of weapons we delivered to you."

"I decided I was going to plan it with no chance of error or risk."

"The Mexicans are going crazy. They said the scene looks like multiple SEAL teams were involved. We of course confirmed no SEAL teams or US military were involved. The Mexican military did confirm they saw no evidence of any breech of their border or air space that would have been necessary for a US military strike. I understand POTUS had to call the president of Mexico to assure him this action was not conducted by any US military."

"I can confirm El Jefe is definitely dead. He survived the claymores but had suffered multiple wounds. I put a round in his head."

"The photos are making the circuit at the highest level in Langley, and I understand they made it to POTUS."

Alan took a few minutes to tell Robert the governor gangway story; Robert could not stop laughing.

"That would have been inconvenient," Robert said after he recovered. "Before I sign off, I want to give you an FYI. We got the list of visitor passes into Puerto Cabello on the day you were there and the day after. There were only nine visitor passes issued over the two days. The syndicate is offering a reward of two hundred thousand US dollars for information. We have also identified the two security guards; both were strong-arm enforcers and killers for the Venezuelan crime syndicate. The bottom line is I want you on full alert. You certainly had a good reason to be at the port, but I don't like the low number of visitors over the two days."

"Roger that. Can we trust our port security contact?"

"We believe we can, but a two-hundred-thousand-dollar cash reward is of course a concern. He has continued providing all the information, so we believe he will be reliable. Blowing your cover could also raise questions on how he knew the information. We have given him one hundred thousand dollars for his work helping you to reduce any temptation."

"OK. Let me know if you hear anything else. Let's hope he doesn't decide to gamble and add another two hundred thousand," Alan replied with concern before they signed off.

Alan was beginning to dread going to New York for the annual marine insurance black-tie dinner the next week. He had meetings with the New York staff of Sea Secure and George, so he could not change his mind. It was going to be very difficult to go back to New York without Maria.

The rest of the week was quiet, but Alan decided to change his very predictable schedule. He ran and bodysurfed at Ocean Beach rather than in Condado. He was on full alert for any signs of surveillance. He also wore his ankle quick-draw holster with the Berretta Tomcat pistol to work and carried the pistol in a backpack when he went to the beach.

Alan flew into LaGuardia on Thursday; the town car was waiting to take him to the Vista Hotel in the World Trade Center. George had made sure Alan had a round-trip first-class ticket.

Friday he spent all day in meetings with New York staff. Alan also had lunch with George in "heaven," the executive dining room on the forty-first floor, with full-length windows overlooking the East River and all of Manhattan.

George, a big stout man with silver hair always dressed in hand tailored suits, was waiting at his usual table. He stood up and shook Alan's hand. George pushed the button on the table, and the waiter in a tux and white gloves immediately came to the table. "Bring us a bottle of the new chardonnay from Cakebread. Alan, how was your trip up?"

"Fine. Thank you for the upgrade."

"No problem. How are you doing?"

"I get better every day. I did start to dread coming to New York without Maria, but the busy day has taken care of that. Is your wife coming tonight?"

"Jean would not miss seeing you. You're the son she never had."

"Great. It will be a pleasure to see her again."

At the end of the lunch, perfectly cooked swordfish, George presented Alan the Chairman's Award plaque and the envelope with the bonus check and said, "Well done. Keep up the great work."

After lunch, George and Alan both went back to finish the meetings before the end of the day.

Getting through the cocktail party and black-tie dinner was harder than Alan had expected. He sat at the table with George and Jean. Jean was interested in learning more about Puerto Rico. She was a real pleasure and listened intently very interested in Alan's island life. After dinner, the cocktail room was reopened with a band. Alan spent about thirty-five minutes and had a drink with George and Jean. Several women tried to get Alan out on the dance floor, but he politely declined. He did dance the twist with Jean before he left and they had fun. Alan let George know he was flying out in the morning and left to catch a cab back to the hotel.

Alan decided to have one more nightcap at the Greatest Bar on Earth on the 107th floor of the World Trade Center before turning in. The bar was half full. He sat at the bar, untied his bow-tie, and unbuttoned his top button. He ordered a Glenmorangie single malt neat with a water back. *I'll be glad to get back to Puerto Rico and take a long run and bodysurf tomorrow.*

Alan was deep in thought when he noticed someone was pulling the bar chair out right next to him. He turned and found himself looking straight into the emerald-green eyes of a beautiful tall blonde in a very short dress. "Mind if I sit here?"

"No. Help yourself."

"So what are you, a waiter, maître d', or a big-band leader?" she replied, barely able to keep a straight face.

Alan turned and examined her carefully. She was probably in her midtwenties, with a beautiful smile and a very athletic build.

"No. So what are you, a Rockette?"

"OK, touché. Your tuxedo threw me off," she said with a smile and a laugh.

"I'm just a businessman in town for a mandatory black-tie dinner. Now it's your turn. What are you drinking?"

"I would like a dirty Absolut martini straight up. Since you look like James Bond, I will have to say shaken, not stirred."

Alan ordered the drink and then turned and smiled. She was extremely attractive, a very beautiful woman.

"I'm Liz. I'm an assistant treasurer for a high-tech company out of Silicon Valley. I'm here meeting with our New York bankers on a bond we plan to issue. So do I look like a CPA?"

"No, you don't. I'm Alan. I'm a marine consultant and currently an expatriate in Puerto Rico."

"Do you dance?"

"Of course."

"I know a great club; let's go dance!"

"I don't dance much lately."

"Well, then it is time you did. It's good for your soul."

"What kind of music?"

"One of my favorite bands, the Neville Brothers from New Orleans, is playing."

"OK, you sold me. I'm from New Orleans, and I actually knows those guys," he said before he asked for and signed the bar bill. They discussed their favorite Neville Brother songs as they finished their drinks.

The small club was in SoHo. It was an excellent venue for an intimate concert. Alan brought Liz backstage to meet the band. They had Heinekens before going out to the dance floor for the concert. Liz was an excellent dancer; as the night progressed, it became more obvious how it would end. They ended up in Liz's room; the sex was very athletic with an edge. After an hour, they both lay sated, out of breath.

Finally Alan stirred and sat up. "I have an early flight and still have to pack. I had a great time, Liz. Here's my business card in case you ever make it down to Puerto Rico."

"Here's my business card if you make it out to San Francisco. I really hope we get to see each other again. How often do you get to New York?"

"I come up just a couple of times a year for meetings."

"OK. Let me know the next time you come, as I am out here a lot. I hope you'll consider San Francisco for a vacation. Let me know, and I'll take some time off and show you around."

"You are a sweetheart," Alan replied, giving her a kiss before he got up and got dressed.

Liz lay in bed watching him. He was tanned and chiseled, with white lines on his body that were definitely scars. He finally slipped on his jacket, gave her a quick kiss, and left to go to his room.

Liz took one more look at Alan's athletic frame. He moved with confidence and a slight swagger. There was a dangerous edge to Alan, and the scars added to this feeling she could not clearly explain. This had been a really interesting night. Normally, she was the one making an excuse to leave at the end of a night.

Alan's town car was waiting in the morning; the traffic on Saturday was light to LaGuardia. Alan was slightly hung over, so he ordered a Bloody Mary once he was settled in his first-class seat. He sat thinking about the previous night with Liz. She was a beautiful woman—smart, confident, and obviously successful. But at this moment, all he could think of was how much he missed Maria and last year's black-tie dinner. It was still too early for any type of relationship. He was sure of that.

CHAPTER 5

GOOD TO BE BACK IN PUERTO RICO

There were no CIA assignments for the next month. Alan had been on alert after the Venezuela assignment, but there were no signs he was being tracked.

Alan was at his desk the day after Three Kings' Day, a holiday in Puerto Rico, when his pager went off. The page was from Robert's contact number at Langley, so he gave him a call.

"You will have a package delivered tomorrow," Robert informed him. "I am sure you are familiar with the coup in 1979 in Grenada by the New Jewel Movement. This communist movement was sponsored by the Cubans. The constitution was suspended, and Bishop took over. Bishop is now in a power struggle with another member of his party. Meanwhile, the Cubans are building a very big runway that will be able to handle any class of military aircraft, including fully loaded bombers. The runway length is much longer than required for commercial airliners, now or for the future. The Cubans have also deployed a full brigade in Grenada with antiaircraft, armored vehicles, artillery, and more. Looks like another coup is in the future, and the relationship is getting stronger between the Cubans and Russians. We need someone with a cover to give us an on-the-ground assessment."

"That's a small island with almost no tourism now. I'll stand out like a sore thumb."

"Roger that. The government of Grenada is buying some critical parts for their primary power plant. They are going to two separate locations that will allow a real good look at the areas where the Cubans and the Russians are stationed. We will arrange for the components to be damaged before they are crated. They will be shipped and insured by Sea Secure to provide your way in and ability to get to both sites. The crates will show no damage, so they will have to be delivered to the site and opened before the damage is discovered. You will fly in to inspect the damaged components for Sea Secure. Reportedly, there are now North Koreans, East Germans, and even Libyans on the island."

"I'll do what I can."

"We are shipping the damaged parts out today, and they should be on site in approximately two weeks. We will call you the day before you have to leave."

They signed off, and Alan finished his day and left the office at 6:00 p.m. He was the last person out. At his condo, he changed into his running clothes and shoes and headed one block over to Luchetti Park for a two-mile run. It was a beautiful early evening with a trade wind blowing and the sun close to setting. Alan was halfway finished with his run when he noticed the plain white van next to the park sidewalk had not moved. The van had pulled up when Alan started his run, and the driver and a passenger had never gotten out of the van.

As Alan was approaching the van for the second time, he noticed the sliding door on the side of the van was cracked slightly open. Alan was still twenty-five yards away. He quickly planted, turned, and began a full sprint back toward his condo. He turned once and saw the van had taken off quickly and made a left turn at the corner, heading in the same direction as his condo. Alan continued a full sprint and made it to the condo door before the van had turned the corner onto Ashford Avenue, where his condo was located. Alan waited inside the condo's tinted-glass door as the van passed slowly with its occupants looking up and down the street. The driver and passenger were definitely South Americans in the forties.

The condo doorman was reading a newspaper behind his desk and had only looked up briefly when Alan came in.

"John, I don't want any guests tonight. I've got a lot of work to finish."

"No problem, Alan. I won't bother you. I'll tell anyone that may stop off that you're not in."

Alan took the elevator up to his condo, where he pulled his Berretta and three extra magazines out of his wall safe. The Berretta already had a magazine, and Alan racked a round into the chamber. Alan immediately called Robert in Langley.

"Robert here."

Alan explained in detail what had just occurred and gave Robert the license plate and descriptions of the van, driver, and passenger.

"I stopped believing in coincidences in 'Nam. I've been worried since I saw the short list of visitors at Puerto Cabello for the Venezuela assignment," Robert said with concern.

"I have no doubt these guys were going to try a grab job on me the next time I ran pass the van. That slightly opened side door was a dead giveaway. That is our exact protocol so the sliding side door can be opened as quickly as possible."

"Roger that. I completely agree. Do you want us to send over backup?"

"No, I am fine. They've lost the element of surprise. I'll be on full alert. I'll be carrying now all the time, and I'll also always have my Department of Defense special agent credentials badge in case I have to use my Berretta."

"Agreed. Do whatever you need to do to stay safe. I have to seriously reconsider sending you to Grenada. I don't want to send you into the lion's den if this is the Cubans or Russians and they know your cover. We may have to send someone else to be safe."

"Let me know what the guys at Langley find out about the van or anything that might fit with the descriptions of the two men." They signed off.

Alan sat on a chair on his tenth floor balcony overlooking the beach. *Great. Now I have to be on full alert all the time. I expect work will be safe—too many people—but I'll have to be extra careful at the parking garage. No more runs or bodysurfing until Langley gets back.*

Alan pulled his DOD badge and his shoulder holster, with the silencer, out of his safe and then got a Windbreaker out of his closet. *A test run to the bakery two blocks down Ashford will be good recon.* He still had his running clothes and shoes on, so he would be ready to move quickly if needed.

Alan told John, the doorman, he was going to get a Cubano and asked if he wanted anything from the bakery. John thanked him but let Alan know he had brought his dinner. Alan headed out for the bakery; he was on full alert and did a scan up and down the block after stepping out the door. The van was nowhere in sight. Traffic was busy, as was typical at this time of night on Ashford Avenue. Alan carefully scanned all the pedestrians as he briskly walked to the bakery. No alarms went off, and he picked up his Cubano sandwich and returned to his condo without incident.

The telephone was ringing when he walked in the condo.

"Alan here."

"We've run the plates, and the van is a Hertz rental picked up yesterday at the airport. Our IT guys are checking the entire incoming airline-passenger and immigration lists to see if we pick up any leads. Standby; we will be getting back to you in about two hours."

"Excellent. I just went a couple of blocks and got a sandwich for dinner. I didn't see the van or any other persons of concern."

"Stay in. We'll get back as soon as we run the passenger lists," Robert said before signing off.

Two and a half hours later the telephone rang.

"We found some persons of interest. Four male passengers, thirty to forty years old, had flown in from Caracas, Venezuela. All four men entered, one after the other, with the same immigration officer at the airport—evidence they were traveling together. One of the men rented the van, and one of the others was registered as an alternate driver with Hertz. We have tracked them, and they are staying at the La Concha Hotel two blocks away from your condo. We ran each man in all the databases, and they're members of a Venezuelan crime syndicate—enforcers and assassins. The syndicate is heavily involved in smuggling, drugs, prostitution, money laundering, and murder. We are ninety percent confirmed this is the syndicate that was handling the arms shipment for FARC. This may just be the smugglers from Puerto Cabello after you, we hope."

"Certainly looks encouraging. Never thought I would be glad to just have a crime syndicate after me. Do you want me to handle these guys?"

"No. We don't want you operating in Puerto Rico—too great of a risk to your cover and the Absolute Resolution program. We'll send a team to pick these guys up, and we'll figure out a federal charge we can pin on them to keep them. We'll have them flown to a quiet place so we can have a chat and find out exactly why they were tracking you. We should have them later tonight and will fly them up as soon as we get them. I'll send you a page as soon as we have all four of them in custody."

"Thanks. I'll await your page," Alan said before signing off.

Two hours later Alan's pager went off. Alan called, and Robert picked up right away. "We got all four. No shots fired. They're on the way to the airport, and we'll give you an update tomorrow."

"Thanks," Alan said. Now it was time for a glass of wine. He slept with the Berretta under the pillow.

The next morning Alan was packing his briefcase to leave work when his pager went off. He called right away.

"They broke quickly," Robert said, "and it certainly appears we're just dealing with the smugglers and the crime syndicate. We're still checking, but I wanted to get you this preliminary information."

"Great. Let's hope this fully checks out. I'll stay on full alert for the next several days."

"Roger that. Grenada assignment is currently estimated for arrival of the damaged components in eight days. We will know by then. If there are any doubts, we will send a company guy as an independent marine consultant to complete the recon work."

After they signed off, Alan sat back down staring out the sliding glass balcony door. *Wonderful. Now I have a price on my head by a major Venezuelan crime syndicate, and they know where I work and live. This is a game changer.*

CHAPTER 6

GRENADA

The next week was quiet, with no signs of any more Venezuelan bad guys. Alan had traveled to Guayama on the South Shore of Puerto Rico to do a preliminary review for a chemical-plant movement. He brought Miguel, who had helped on the pressboard factory move, to complete the assignment.

On the drive back, Alan's pager went off, and he pulled off Highway 52 to use a pay telephone.

Robert picked up on the first ring. "Well, we have good news. Due to the critical nature of the recent events, we used lie-detector tests and drugs on the four Venezuelans. One was a top leader in the syndicate. They were to receive a half million US dollars for smuggling the arms shipment to Colombia. The Cubans and Russians believed they were sold out by the syndicate and did not pay them. They believed the syndicate sold the shipment information to the US and Colombian governments. The syndicate of course denied they had, but now the Russians and Cubans will not use them anymore. They have found a different crime syndicate; there is no shortage of crime syndicates and smugglers in Venezuela. The syndicate saw that an American had visited the port, and they decided they would kidnap you, torture you, and make you confess you were an agent of the US government. They were then planning to kill you. They had no idea you were actually a US government agent; they thought they would be blaming an innocent US citizen. They have not turned your name over to the Cuban, Russians, or Colombians."

"Sometimes the truth is stranger than fiction. So our interrogation guys feel good on this story?"

"Our top guys feel very strongly that they have extracted the correct information. The men's statements tied together, with only the few normal contradictions. Everyone knows how critical this is for your safety. We can indict all four of the Venezuelans on drug-smuggling charges, so they are not going anywhere."

"OK. I'll stay on alert in case they send any more guys."

"Roger that. The shipments have also arrived in Grenada, and we are expecting the call for the cargo claims shortly. I think you are good to go on this one. How do you feel?"

"If our top guys are confident on the interrogation results, I am good to go."

"Great. You are by far our best asset for this work, given your military background. I'll have the claim call relayed to your office when it comes in."

The next day the claim report was received by telex in the Sea Secure office; Ana created a file and brought it into Alan's office. "Boss, we have a new set of claims in Grenada. Who do you want to handle them?"

"I'll handle them. I'll let Miguel continue working on the chemical-plant movement."

"OK. I'll make your airline, hotel, and car reservations for tomorrow," she said as she handed him the file.

***

Alan left in the morning and had to connect through Miami to reach Grenada and arrived in the late afternoon. The flight to

Grenada was nearly empty, with only a handful of passengers. The negative press on the coup was adversely affecting tourism.

Alan waited in line at immigration and customs, both completed at the same time. When it was his turn, he handed the immigration officer his passport and laid his carry-on bag on the folding table for customs. The immigration officer carefully examined all the stamps in Alan's passport for several minutes. "Please stand over here, Mr. Joubert."

"Is there a problem with my passport?"

"Just stand over here."

In a few minutes, a man in plain clothes with a pistol asked Alan to follow him. Alan was brought into a small room with a table and two chairs. "Put your bag on the table," the man commanded.

Alan complied, and the man immediately unzipped the bag and dumped Alan's clothes on the dirty floor. He searched through the clothes, using his foot to spread them out. "Put your briefcase on the table."

"I have an expensive camera. Please be careful."

"Why do you need an expensive camera? Are you a tourist?"

"No. I'm here on business. Your government received some components for your power plant repair, and they arrived damaged. I'm here to examine the damage and provide a report for your insurance claim."

The man carefully examined everything in the briefcase. There was nothing but the camera, the files for the cargo claims, business cards, notepad, a calculator, and a gold Cross pen and mechanical pencil set.

"Pick up your clothes and put them in your bag. Then follow me."

The man led Alan back to immigration and customs, which was now empty of passengers. "Stamp his passport. He has a three-day limit."

Alan's passport was stamped, and as he walked out, the men started to joke and laugh as the man told them what he had just done.

Alan picked up his rental car and drove to the hotel in St. George's. He called the general manager of the power plant, his contact, and set up one inspection in St. George's for that day and the inspection of the other cargo in Calivigny for the next day. Alan completed the first inspection and then met with the general manager, whose office was at this site. The general manager was happy with the results; the component was a total loss, and Alan would recommend it be replaced.

"I really want to go bodysurfing this afternoon. Is there a good beach nearby?" Alan asked as he packed up his briefcase.

"The best surfing beaches are on the northeast end of the island. There are smaller waves and a very beautiful beach at Grand Anse Beach. It is a tourist attraction."

"Thanks; please let your manager in Calivigny know I'll be there tomorrow at ten o'clock. Thank you for your cooperation."

Alan drove around St. George's, collecting intel on troop and equipment deployment and barracks locations. He did not write anything down in case he was searched when he was departing immigration and customs. After he had driven and walked the city for an hour and a half, he dropped off his briefcase and changed at his hotel. Then he went bodysurfing at the recommended beach. The beach was beautiful. Small waves, perfect for an amphibious landing. Alan took photos of the entire beach.

The next morning Alan completed the inspection of the damaged switching gear, and he declared it a total loss, requiring replacement. The inspection took less than an hour. Alan started his "sightseeing" drive up the east coast, completing a recon of Marquis and Grenville before heading back across the island to return to St. George's. He was just passing Mount Saint Catherine when a car with a flashing red light on the dash pulled him over.

Two men got out and approached Alan's car. Both men were in plain clothes and looked very athletic. The first man commanded Alan to get out of the car. "What are you doing out here?" he asked sharply.

"I had business here that is finished. Just want to see the island. I have never been here before. You have a beautiful island."

"Get out of the car," the man who was obviously in charge demanded.

"What is the problem, sir? I was not speeding, and I was driving responsibly."

Both men were now standing several feet away from Alan's door. He slowly got out and measured each large athletic man, deciding how he would take them both out.

"Give me your driver's license. Where is your camera? Give us your camera," the team leader demanded.

"Why do you want my camera?" Alan responded. He gave the man his Louisiana driver's license instead of his Puerto Rico driver's license.

"If we have to ask you again, you will be under arrest. Give me your camera." Alan started to open the back rear door to get his briefcase. The team leader grabbed Alan's arm and pushed him away; the other man pulled his pistol, opened the door, and grabbed the briefcase. "Stand right where you are, and do not move."

The team leader opened the briefcase on the rear trunk and removed Alan's camera. He rewound the roll of film and then opened the camera and pulled the film roll out. He searched the briefcase for any other film rolls.

"We will follow you back to your hotel. You are to remain in your hotel until you leave. We will develop your film and provide you your photos at the airport before you leave tomorrow."

The next morning Alan returned his rental car and was at the airport an hour early for his flight. He had not taken any photos of the military operations so he didn't expect any trouble. At Immigration and Customs agents again pulled him into the same small room. His clothes were again dumped on the floor and kicked around. They examined everything in his briefcase, including all his files and notepads. When they finished, Alan was told to repack his bag.

"Good-bye, Mr. Joubert. We hope you enjoyed your stay and our hospitality," the team leader said as he handed Alan an envelope of developed photos. The team leader and the two men with him laughed and led Alan to the gate.

CHAPTER 7

GRENADA INTEL

Alan flew back to Puerto Rico, connecting through Miami. He drove to his condo and called Robert in Langley as soon as he got in.

Alan explained to Robert everything that had happened and advised he would provide a detailed recon report.

"There was a full Cuban brigade, Russian combat and engineering companies, and several hundred North Koreans. The works. I even saw what I am sure was a Libyan. I drove by the runway they are building, and it could take off and land a B52. I'll telex the detailed report later tomorrow."

"You showed great restraint. It must have been tough to smile through all that abuse. So glad you did not take the two men down on the road; I have no doubt you could have if necessary."

"If and when we go back in force, I want to attend. I have an excellent lay of the land, and it would be enjoyable."

"Roger that. Your work on the ground verifies a great deal of our intel. I expect there will be fireworks there in the future if this military buildup continues. This has turned into a silent invasion by the Cubans and Russians, aided by local corrupt help. We are not going to sit around and let them create a strategic bomber base a hundred miles from South America. Especially with a large groundswell of support by the majority of citizens in Grenada who want to end the coup and return to a democracy. The locals want to get back to being a tourist destination and having free elections. They just don't stand a chance against heavily armed and well-trained Cubans and Russians."

"I think the general manager of the power plant may have called the guys who stopped me, as he was eyeing me very carefully in our meeting. That added to their suspicion at my arrival. I believe they also wanted to give an American grief. They did make sure I had no written intel or photos that would indicate I was something other than a businessman. If I had, I expect I would still be there."

***

Alan got to the office early to telex his detailed recon report to Robert. He then sat at his desk to take care of the issues that had stacked up while he was traveling. Ana popped her head in at 8:30 a.m.

"How was your trip, boss?"

"No problems. I'll get you the reports this afternoon. All of the cargo was a total loss and will have to be replaced. Do you have anything else, other than this stack on my desk?"

"No. Sonia did call yesterday and asked you to call. I have a couple of other telephone messages I'll bring back in a few minutes."

"Excellent," Alan replied with a smile.

Alan called Sonia first.

"Alan, I am determined to get you out to a beach party this Saturday. It will be just a bunch of friends; most were friends of Maria. It will be at a great house right on the beach in Isla Verde."

"What time does it start?"

"It starts around eight in the evening. It will be fun. There will be a salsa band, torches, and a great swimming pool—besides, it's right on the beach."

"OK, I'll stop by. See you there about nine."

"Great. See you then," Sonia said before they signed off.

It is time to get out and go to a party, Alan mused. *I think it is time.*

Alan had finished for the day and was heading to the multi-story parking garage a block away when he noted the tail care-less following too close with obvious interest. There was no doubt about it. The man was far from professional. Alan stopped at a local shop across the street from the garage to pick up a *San Juan Star,* the local English-language newspaper. The man awkwardly waited across the street, in full view from the store.

OK, looks like the crime syndicate has sent reinforcements; no doubt they will try to grab me in the parking garage. How many men will be there? Alan walked over to the pay telephone in the corner and called Robert's number. "Looks like I have crime-syndicate bad guys again. Got a really unprofessional tail that followed me when I left my office af-ter work; I was heading to the parking garage to get my car."

"Where are you now?"

"I'm across the street from the parking garage in a small store."

"The Federal Building is two blocks away. I can send a couple of FBI guys who park in the same garage."

"I need one FBI agent to scout my car right away. If there are no more than two men, have him leave it to me. I'll need help from a cleaner afterward."

"Roger that. I'll get someone from the FBI SWAT team over to the garage for a recon. Go back to your office so it looks like you forgot something, and I'll page you."

"My car is on the third floor right next to the elevator. The parking spot is marked 'Manager of Sea Secure.'"

Robert quickly signed off, and Alan left the store and briskly headed back to his office a block away. Out of the corner of his eye, he could see his tail was confused but again followed him back to the office. Alan entered his office building and caught the elevator up to his office.

Thirty minutes later Alan's pager went off. He called Robert immediately.

"One of the top FBI SWAT leaders did a recon at the parking garage. Your tail is still waiting for you outside your building. There is one other guy waiting next to a parked car four parking places down from yours. There is also a white van with at least two guys, parked with its hazard lights blinking. The FBI just ran the plates, and it's another Hertz rental from the San Juan airport. Looks positively like a repeat, and they're after you again. The FBI SWAT guy is really top-notch. He's an ex-marine. He has requested to accidentally hit the van with his car to damage the side sliding door so he would have a reason to ask for their insurance and driver's licenses. I like it; it buys us time."

"Sounds like a plan. I have my ankle Tomcat Berretta. Let's coordinate, and I can get up there at the same time. I either drive away, or we have a gun battle with these guys, and all the action can be attributed to an accident with an FBI agent that resulted in a shootout. That will cover-up I was also shooter."

"I like it. But I'll make one change to even the odds. I'll have the FBI SWAT guy bring a partner. When I page you, it will be mark fifteen minutes ETA to the FBI arrival at your car."

Ten minutes later Alan's pager went off. He pulled his Tomcat ankle Berretta out of his ankle quick-draw holster, checked the seven-round magazine, and chambered a round. He set his dive watch bezel on fourteen minutes and then locked the office and took the elevator down. When he exited the building, he picked up the tail right away. Alan took a quick glance at his watch; right on schedule.

Alan reached the parking garage and took the stairs up to the third floor. His tail followed him up the stairs, staying one floor below him. When Alan opened the stairwell door, he could see a tall athletic South American man leaning against a car three down from his and the white van with the blinking hazard lights.

He checked his watch just as he heard a car coming around the corner. The Ford Crown Victoria struck the side of the van, heavily damaging the side sliding door. The FBI agents quickly exited their car and walked back to the van.

"Sorry, but what are you doing parking in the driveway behind parked cars?" the lead FBI SWAT man said in an irritated tone.

The man three cars down began walking toward the van. Alan ducked behind the wall next to his car as the tail man opened the door and walked toward the van.

The driver got out of the van. "You hit my van, and you will have to pay for it."

"No problem. I'll give you my insurance and my driver's license number, and you give me the same."

At that moment the driver saw the radio antenna on the Ford Crown Victoria and started to draw his gun. The tail and the man who had been waiting by Alan's car started approaching the FBI SWAT agents from behind. They reached into their jackets and drew their pistols. Alan immediately pulled his ankle Berretta out and fired two rounds each to the heads of the two crime-syndicate men. One FBI SWAT agent drew his pistol and gunned down the van driver before he could get a shot off. The van passenger got one round off before he was hit by multiple rounds from the second FBI SWAT agent. One of the FBI SWAT agents pulled the back door of the van open while the other man waited, ready to fire. The back of the van was empty. The crime syndicate had again sent a four-man team.

The lead FBI SWAT agent quickly walked over to Alan. "Thanks for covering our backs. The powers that be want you out of here right away. We're going to write this up as a car accident. There were bad guys from another country, and it escalated. There will be no mention of you."

"Roger that. Thanks for the first-class support," Alan replied before jogging over to his car. He exited the garage and was a half block away when three San Juan police cars pulled up with their lights on but no sirens. Six policemen, two with M16s, jumped out of the police cars and ran into the garage.

Alan called Robert when he got to his condo.

"What happened?" Robert asked.

"The FBI SWAT guys were excellent. No one left to arrest. I got out clean, and there are no cameras in the garage. Fortunately no civilians were around. We took out four; I got two."

"Let me think this over moving forward. I was surprised they tried to get you again. We obviously can't have this keep happening."

"Well, that would be the understatement of the year," Alan replied with a slight chuckle. Then he signed off.

Alan showered to get rid of the smell of cordite and then drove to the Metropol for dinner. *Thank heavens the tail man was incompetent. I was just starting to relax, and if the tail man had been good today, this could have easily ended differently.*

CHAPTER 8

LION'S DEN

The next morning Alan was in the office early, as usual. He closed his door and called Robert, who picked up on the first ring.

"Alan, the concern now is what will the crime syndicate do next? I'm afraid they may have figured out that they actually picked a government agent. Will they go to the Russians and Cubans and tell them? This would prove they did not sell the shipment out."

"I'm at the same place in the thought process," Alan quietly responded. "I do expect that will happen next, if it has not already happened. The real question is what will the Russians and Cubans do after they are told? It certainly is going to make things more dangerous on some of my missions. I think we will have to weigh this for each assignment that directly involves the Russians and Cubans."

"Speaking of new missions, I'm still waiting on the one I said would be coming, but I was just getting ready to page you when you called. A US tug broke a wire while towing an oil barge off Cuba. The tug and barge are insured by Sea Secure. The Cubans grabbed the barge, which was barely in their waters, and towed it to Puerto Tanamo; the barge and the oil cargo are undamaged. The Cubans have advised the vessel owner they will release the barge, with the oil, for one million US dollars."

"I am surprised the Cubans are willing to release the barge and oil, but imagine they need the U.S dollars more than the barge or trying to sell the oil," Alan interjected.

"I think you are right. Sea Secure wants to send someone to make sure the barge and cargo are undamaged and the barge is ready to be rigged for tow and turned over to the US tug. The Sea Secure manager in New Orleans wants to send you. It went up the ladder to the big boss at Sea Secure, and he called the CIA director," Robert said, waiting for Alan response.

"Well, this is really interesting."

"As you know, you'll need special travel documents to get in and out. Quite frankly, I'm worried about sending you there, what with everything going on with the Venezuelan crime syndicate. How do you feel about going?" Robert asked with concern.

"I have very mixed feelings. If the Cubans know about Puerto Cabello, or maybe even more, I'll be walking into at best a jail cell and at worst an accident after extensive interrogation. The bottom line is I think it's too big a risk for me to go right now until we see how the Venezuelan problem plays out."

"Great. We are in complete agreement. This may be an opportunity to check out any bells your name may ring. I was thinking maybe we let you handle all the details and future telexes to the Cubans, and we send another outside consultant to inspect the barge and cargo for the transfer and tow."

"I'm good handling that, and you're right: maybe it will let us know if my name rings any bells."

The information was telexed to Alan after they signed off. This included the contact numbers for personnel for all the Cuban units involved: the maritime division, finance division, and, of course, the security division. Alan called the maritime division contact first. They discussed in detail the condition of the barge, towing bridle, and oil cargo. Everything was undamaged, and the barge was ready to be towed and transferred to the US tug. The operation would require good weather; and light winds and seas were predicted for the week.

"When are you arriving to complete your inspection?" the maritime contact asked.

"We have a marine consultant flying out of New Orleans. He will connect through Mexico City to fly into Havana tomorrow," Alan advised.

"You aren't coming yourself?"

"No. I'm tied up with other issues but will handle the details and arrange for the money wire by Sea Secure and the vessel owner."

"I was told by my security division contact you would be coming. I think you should call him next."

"He'll be my next call. Thanks for all your help."

"You're welcome. Your Spanish is excellent for a *Norteamericano*," he said before saying good-bye.

Alan sat back in his chair and stared out his window at the harbor. The next call would be interesting.

Alan dialed the number of Captain Rodriguez of the security division. Alan was put on hold for several minutes.

"Captain Rodriguez," he answered when he picked up the line.

"This is Alan Joubert of Sea Secure, the marine insurance company for the barge owner. I want to finalize the transfer of the payment and the release of the barge. I just finished speaking with the gentleman at the marine division and plan to call the contact in the finance division after we are finished."

"We understood you will be coming for the barge inspection, Mr. Joubert?"

"No. I'm tied up on other business issues. We're sending an excellent marine consultant to make sure the barge is undamaged and ready to tow. I'll be contacting your finance division to get the bank wiring instructions."

"That's a shame. I was looking forward to meeting you," Captain Rodriguez said in a threatening tone.

"Any other issues before I get the payment information? Our marine consultant will be landing tomorrow afternoon in Havana. We would hope you could arrange a hotel, as well as arrange transport for him to Puerto Tanamo," Alan responded ignoring the obvious threat

"No problem, Mr. Joubert. We will have a driver and security man assigned to your consultant while he is in Cuba. We will make sure we give him all the help he requires for this transfer. Please have the contact from the finance division call me after you have finished your discussion."

"I'll do that, Captain. Thanks for all your help," Alan said, ready to sign off.

"Maybe we will meet at some other time," Captain Rodriguez said coldly before saying good-bye.

Alan called the finance division next and got the wire-transfer information for Sea Secure and the vessel owner's contact information. The Sea Secure policy did not have coverage for ransom, but given the important client relationship with the vessel owner, Sea Secure had agreed to pay $750,000 as a "salvage payment." The vessel owner was to pay the balance of $250,000. Alan explained these details to the Cuban finance contact, a savvy finance guy who completely understood the basis of the payments. Sea Secure had gotten permission to wire the $750,000 directly to the Cuban Finance Division, with the vessel owner wiring the balance. Both wire payments required special approval by the US Department of the Treasury for these normally illegal actions.

Alan next called the vessel owner, who he knew from his time in New Orleans, and then the Sea Secure director of claims to provide the details of the wiring instructions, which he followed up by telex. When Alan was finished, he immediately called Robert.

"Well, I certainly got a not-so-veiled warning from a Captain Rodriguez of the Cuban security unit working on the oil barge's release."

"I was afraid of that. No doubt the Venezuelans have told the Russians and Cubans about losing eight men trying to grab and frame you, proving they were right in the first place."

"The captain signed off by saying, 'Maybe we might meet at some other time,'" Alan replied with a laugh.

"He'd better hope not. It could be detrimental to his health and future retirement. OK, finish this oil barge project, and then plan on coming up to Langley for a few days so we can talk about the best ways to deal with this new threat moving forward."

The next day the marine consultant confirmed that the barge and cargo were undamaged and the bridle was ready to accept a tow wire once the barge was delivered to the US tug. The Sea Secure third-party marine consultant planned to ride the barge out and come back with the US tug. Once the barge left, Alan arranged for Sea Secure to wire its portion and sent a telex to the vessel owner to wire his portion. In approximately four hours, the marine consultant called Alan by very high frequency (VHF) by way of the maritime international operator. He advised that the barge had been taken in tow by the US tug and was now in international waters. A US Navy frigate was waiting and had taken up escort at that point. It would remain with them until they reached US waters.

The next morning Alan was in his office when he received a telex from Sea Secure confirming the bank wire of its portion, but he did not have one from the vessel owner. He sent a brief telex to the vessel owner asking for confirmation of the transfer.

After an hour Ana came back to Alan's office holding a telex. "You're not going to like this, boss," she said quietly and handed

Alan the telex. It was from the tug and barge owner, and it was a short message: "Fuck Castro. He pirated my oil barge; I am not going to pay him a nickel."

Alan called the Sea Secure director of claims and left a message that the barge owner was not going to pay.

He next called Robert. "Well, we've got a new twist. The barge owner reneged on their two hundred fifty thousand US dollars to the Cubans."

"You have got to be kidding."

"You can't make this stuff up. I got a telex from the barge owner stating 'Fuck Castro.'"

"Well now, this is not going to raise your popularity in Cuba," Robert said, chuckling.

"Well, you know me: always go out with a bang, literally and figuratively. I'll fly up Monday; I have to catch up here at Sea Secure."

"Keep on alert."

"You can bet the ranch on that," Alan said before signing off.

Ana buzzed back after he hung up. "There's a woman named Liz who said you would know who she was."

"Thanks, Ana. Pass her back."

Alan picked up the line. "Alan here."

"Hi, Alan. Hope you're doing well."

"All is good. How are you, Liz?"

"I'm doing great. Busy as always, working sixty hours a week. I've been awarded an all-expenses-paid, seven-day vacation at the Jamaica Inn in Ocho Rios, Jamaica. My boss is trying to get me to throttle down for a week after my big successful bond deal. I raised one billion at two basis points under our goal."

"Great job, and congratulations."

"I was hoping you could take some time off and come. They reserved the White Suite, a private cottage with its own swimming pool and private beach."

"Wow, that sounds amazing. What time frame are you considering?"

"This coming month," she replied hopefully.

"Let me check my schedule and get back to you. Thanks for thinking of me. I'll get back by Friday to see if I can make it work. Sounds like fun."

"Great. Here's my home number so you can call me at the office or home," she replied and gave Alan the number.

"Thanks for the offer, and talk soon," Alan said. "Bye."

Liz sat at her desk, staring out her office window overlooking South San Francisco Bay. This was the first man she'd ever had to call back.

Ana waited until Alan was off the telephone before she knocked on his office door. "Boss, we have a loss off Culebra. New York would like you to handle it. A privately owned ex-navy vessel—they called it an LST—ran aground off Culebra. It was carrying forty-two Dodge K-cars owned by a big rental-car company. The vessel has reportedly flooded, and the cars are partially underwater. Sea Secure insures the cars, and they were to be delivered to Saint Croix. Here is the latitude and longitude."

Alan pulled out the chart of Culebra and plotted the position. "Call Pedro and set up his seaplane. Give him the latitude and longitude; I'm sure he can land."

This type of assignment was Alan's favorite part of his Sea Secure work. When he hung up, he ordered a derrick barge and a deck barge to the site to recover the cars.

***

Alan landed by seaplane and reviewed the vessel and cargo. Cars were flooded with saltwater halfway up the doors. The derrick barge got there in five hours, as it was in the area with the deck cargo barge. Alan supervised the offloading of the forty-two Dodge K-cars, and then departed. The vessel was not his problem.

The cars were delivered back to San Juan and stored on a pier. Alan turned the claim over to Miguel to close out the disposition of the cars and complete the report.

CHAPTER 9

LANGLEY, THE BAHAMAS, AND JAMAICA

Alan flew into Dulles airport, and the driver with his name board was waiting to pick him up and take him directly to Langley. Alan had a CIA ID, so he passed directly through security and took the elevator up to Robert's office on the sixth floor. Eileen, his secretary, asked Alan to wait; Robert was wrapping up a conference call and would be available shortly.

Within minutes, Robert invited Alan in and offered him a chair. "Good to see you, Alan. Thanks for coming up. I was just on a conference call with the top man. We're very concerned about your safety. We've been working on the intelligence to determine what we could about your exposure. Unfortunately, no news is not good news. We have determined you have become a target of both Russian and Cuban intelligence, as well as still being an active target of the Venezuelan crime syndicate."

"Wow. Do you have any good news?"

"Yes. You get to take two weeks' vacation off the grid somewhere. We really would like it to be off the grid—not a large city, and definitely not Puerto Rico."

"OK, so if I do that, what is going to magically happen that takes me out of the bull's-eye for the Russians and the Cubans?"

"We're working on a smokescreen that discredits the intel the Venezuelan crime syndicate provided to the Russians and Cubans. No need to share the details, but we are setting up actions and facts that prove you were not responsible for the lost arms shipment. We believe we can steer the Russians and Cubans off course. The Venezuelan cartel is a different story. If and when we succeed and lead the Russians and Cubans away from you, we will look at an Absolute Resolution for the head of the Venezuelan crime syndicate and its top members."

"I sure hope your plan works," Alan replied in a concerned quiet tone, leaning back in his chair. "I really like Puerto Rico now, and I sure don't want to be on full combat alert twenty-four hours per day. I have been invited on a one-week vacation in Jamaica by a woman I recently met in New York. I could do one week with her, and I can then go see my ex-marine recon buddy, a security man on a billionaire's yacht. Once this blew up, I contacted him. The yacht is anchored in the Bahamas, and the owner will not be back on board for two weeks."

"Where and how did you meet the woman?" Robert asked with concern.

"In New York when I was up for the back-tie dinner for the marine insurance industry to receive the Chairman's Award from my company. I checked her out. Liz is twenty-seven years old and works at a Fortune 100 high-tech firm in the Silicon Valley outside of San Francisco. She is an assistant treasurer and was in New York completing a bond deal. She's a Yale graduate with a degree in finance and an MBA in business management. She's very beautiful, smart, and successful woman. I have already checked the hotel in Jamaica, and they have armed security guys who are retired from the Special Air Service. The hotel is very high-end."

"Ok, but I still plan to have the backroom guys check her out," Robert replied.

"Roger that. In the Bahamas, I couldn't be in a safer place in the world than with Fast Eddie on the yacht. Fast Eddie was my sniper in my marine recon unit. It would be a real tactical error for my stalkers to show up when I'm visiting Eddie."

"Excellent; sounds like we have a great plan to take you off the grid. The top guy has made it very clear to all of us what he expects—working to create the smoke screen to get the Russians and Cubans off your trail."

Alan and Robert spent the next several hours talking over all his past jobs and different trails that might get linked together if the Russians and Cubans were really good or lucky. When they finished, Robert stood. "Alan, go ahead and spend the night. Eileen can get you a hotel over at the Radisson near the Pentagon Metro station. I know the last time you were here you wanted to go see the Vietnam Veterans Memorial. It's not quite finished, but it'll be dedicated in November, and we will definitely fly you up for that event. Why don't you take the Metro over to the memorial? Then I can buy you dinner."

"Sounds great," Alan replied as he got up to leave. Robert followed him out and asked Eileen to make Alan's hotel reservation.

Alan took the Metro to the hotel, checked in, and dropped off his bag. Then he caught the Metro back to see the memorial. Alan approached the memorial site from Constitution Avenue. Alan was stunned by the beauty of the polished-granite wall with the etched names of all service personnel killed in action. The images of the surrounding trees reflected off the highly polished black granite. The east end wall pointed directly at the Washington Monument, with the west wall pointing to the Lincoln Memorial. Alan found the names of the two recon team members he had lost, as well as several others he had known in his one and a half tours. This was one of the most powerful experiences Alan had felt since he flew out of 'Nam the last time.

Alan met Robert at 8:00 p.m. for dinner at a very high-end French restaurant in Georgetown. Robert had a Glenmorangie single-malt scotch waiting for him when he sat down. The table was located in a discreet corner in the restaurant. Robert had invited Alan to dinner to catch up on Alan and make sure he was recovering from the loss of the love of his life, Maria.

"No business—how are you doing personally?" Robert asked with concern.

"I'm still really struggling. I'm trying to throw myself into work for the Company and Sea Secure. I am also trying to return to my previous personal schedule of running and bodysurfing, but I just feel empty now. I'm not sure I'll ever love again. I feel guilty for flying off on assignment and not being with her at the meeting when she and her partner were ambushed."

"You have been doing this long enough to know these are all natural feelings," Robert said very quietly with concern leaning toward Alan. "This was all too personal for you. Maria and her partner were going to meet an informant. There were no warning signs. If there were, NCIS would have sent backup. Remember, time will heal all. Don't beat yourself up on this. Do you want counseling from the Company?"

"No, thanks. I don't think it will help, and I don't want that on my record," Alan replied quietly.

"Alan, it will not be a black mark on your record, I assure you."

"No, really, I do appreciate your concern and trying to help. I have to get through this myself. I do believe time will heal. Thanks again, Robert, for your concern."

The rest of the conversation was just small talk before they wrapped it up for the night.

When Alan got back to the hotel, he called Liz.

"How about taking me to Jamaica?" Alan began with a chuckle.

"Alan, I am so glad to hear from you. I am even happier to hear you can make Jamaica."

"Looks like I am going to have some time for a couple of weeks off. Do you have a schedule yet?"

"Yes, I can definitely make it the end of next week. I can't wait to see you again. I do want you to know you're the only man I've ever had to call back after a date," she said with a laugh.

"I'm flattered. I'll be heading off tomorrow for the Bahamas. What day do you want me to fly into Montego Bay?"

"Hold on while I check my American Airlines schedule book. I can catch the red-eye out of San Francisco and get into Montego Bay midday next Tuesday."

"Excellent. Let me know your flight, and I'll be waiting in the airport for you."

"Great! The hotel is sending a car to pick us up at the airport. I understand the White Suite at the Jamaica Inn is one of the top resort destinations in the Caribbean."

They said good-bye, and Alan called Eddie to confirm he would be catching a seaplane tomorrow to where the yacht was anchored in the Great Exuma island chain.

The trip went smoothly, and Alan looked out the windscreen of the seaplane at the magnificent eighty-six-foot Palmer Johnson yacht anchored in the clear blue water. There was also a forty-two-foot Bertram sport fisherman anchored near the yacht. Alan could see Fast Eddie in the nineteen-foot Boston whaler dinghy waiting to pick him up. Once the seaplane landed, Eddie maneuvered the dinghy alongside the seaplane pontoon and Alan transferred his bag and climbed aboard.

Eddie looked great, his six foot one hundred and eighty pound frame was in perfect shape; only his sandy blonde hair was longer than usual. He was only wearing Bermuda shorts, camouflaged boonie hat and sunglasses. Alan could clearly see the white scar from the gunshot wound on Eddie's tanned right shoulder.

Alan was simply amazed when he got to the eighty-six footer—a beautiful vessel with all mahogany woodwork below. He learned the Bertram sport fisherman also belonged to the billionaire; he liked to sport fish, and Eddie was the captain of the sport fisherman when they went fishing.

Alan and Fast Eddie spent the next four days relaxing, drinking Red Stripe beers, diving, windsurfing, and sport fishing. Alan thought back to the days before he signed up for the CIA Absolute Resolution program and was chartering his forty-six-foot ketch in these same breathtaking aquamarine waters. The eighty-six-footer had a crew of a captain; Fast Eddie, the first mate; an engineer; a steward; a hostess; and a great chef. The owner had left the full crew on board, as he was planning on coming back in two weeks. All the crew members were really laid-back and friendly.

The last night Alan and Eddie were sitting by themselves in the aft deck area. The crew had been great and had given them plenty of space.

"Fast Eddie, you have struck gold. What a great life you have. This makes me really miss my old charter days."

"Quit. Come on back to charter work. I can get you a job on one of these beauties in a second."

"Things are bit more complicated now."

"I expected as much. You know if you ever need my help, all you have to do is call. I'll drop everything and be there. I couldn't miss the white lines on your back from when you saved me from the RPG and took all the shrapnel in 'Nam."

"Thanks, Eddie. You know it works both ways. So good to catch up with you, and thanks for this incredible vacation. I have just one question," Alan said with a big smile. "Are you and the hostess hooked up?"

"Piece of cake," he said, and they burst out laughing. He gave Alan a fist bump, and they both pulled back their open hands like an explosion and then saluted.

Alan caught the seaplane out the next morning, with arrangements to catch an American Airlines flight out of Miami International Airport to Montego Bay. Alan's flight arrived an hour before Liz was scheduled to land. He cleared immigration and customs and waited in the bar outside the customs gate, sipping a Red Stripe beer.

A little more than an hour later, the first several passengers from Liz's flight passed through the door from customs. Liz was the fourth passenger out—she had obviously been in first class. She had a porter with a dolly and two large suitcases. She spotted Alan immediately and ran over and gave him a hug and a kiss. "I'm exhausted from the red-eye, but you certainly are a sight for sore eyes. The porter is going out to look for our car. I can't believe we are here in Jamaica."

Liz was wearing shorts, a tube top, and sandals, and her hair was pulled back in a long blond ponytail. She looked stunning, like a fashion model from a magazine.

The Jamaica Inn was an amazing older resort at the beach with old-fashioned service. The White Suite, located right on the beach, was a separate cottage with its own private pool, patio, and beach. The first three days were filled with diving, sailing, bodysurfing, and windsurfing. Liz was very athletic, and she looked stunning in the many different bikinis she had brought for the trip.

They had a great time, and the sex was excellent, but for Alan it was just sex. He still deeply missed Maria, but he did enjoy being with Liz. She was a smart and engaging woman with a keen sense of humor, and it was a real pleasure to spend this time off with her. The conversations were focused on Liz's recent bond deal, living in the Bay Area, and Alan's experiences living in Puerto Rico. The topics were typical of friends spending time together.

On the fourth day, they decided they would go out of the hotel for dinner. The concierge had recommended a French restaurant in Montego Bay, and the hotel arranged for a car. The restaurant was excellent, and they had a gourmet dinner of fresh fish and a superb bottle of French wine. It was a beautiful night with a half moon and a steady trade-wind breeze. Liz said she wanted to walk around and see Montego Bay, so after dinner they took a walk. They spent time looking in store windows and admiring the architecture. After thirty minutes Liz was ready to go back to the restaurant and call for the car.

They were three blocks from the restaurant, on a dark and quiet street, when three Jamaicans came around the corner heading toward them. When the three men were five feet away, they stopped right in front of Alan and Liz. The larger man, slightly behind the other two, spoke first. "Hello. You must be Americans. We are just poor Jamaicans, mon, and we need your help."

Alan pulled ten Jamaican dollars from his wallet. "You bet, guys. Let me buy each of you a Red Stripe," he replied. He reached forward to hand them the bill.

"Sorry. That won't work. We want all of your money, and the lady's jewelry, mon," the leader of the group responded as they all displayed the machetes they had hidden behind their backs.

"Liz, step back five feet," Alan said and turned to make sure she had moved back. Alan then turned slowly and took a step forward. "Listen, guys. We don't want any trouble." Alan was now within two feet of all three men.

"Sorry, boss. We need your cash, credit cards, and the lady's jewelry," the leader said in a threatening manner. "In fact, maybe we will take the young lady for a drink as well."

Alan lunged forward, disarming the closest man and striking his windpipe with his left fist. At the same time, he kicked the second man in the side of his knee. The man struck in the windpipe dropped to his knees and fell forward; the second man collapsed as his knee buckled sideways. He screamed in agony and fell to the ground, holding his leg.

The leader, who was standing slightly behind both of the other men, was paralyzed.

"You have a choice. You can walk away now," Alan said in a cold voice. The third man immediately turned and ran off. Alan walked over and checked the pulse of the first man, whom he had hit in the throat. He had a pulse, and he was breathing. Alan had held back just enough not to kill him; he would definitely need a trip to the hospital, along with the man with the heavily damaged knee.

Alan turned around to check on Liz; she was standing with her mouth open and just starting to recover. Alan went over and wrapped his arms around her, and she began to weep and tremble. "I was so scared; I can't believe you took care of three men with machetes."

"Let's get back to the restaurant and get our car."

When they got back to the restaurant, Alan asked the doorman to call the car, and they returned to the hotel.

"I definitely need a drink—a strong one," Liz said, her voice still shaky.

"Sure. Let's go to the bar," Alan replied as he led her into the beach bar. They ordered drinks, and then there were several minutes of silence.

"Alan, what actually do you do for a living?" Liz said with concern.

"I'm a marine consultant. I was in the military, and I do know how to take care of myself."

"I think that would certainly be an understatement. I have never seen anything like that. Thank heavens you could do it, but the whole thing was terrifying."

"Of course it was; three men with machetes tried to rob us. You have every reason to feel the way you do now."

"Thank you so much for taking care of me. Let's take these drinks back to the room. I want to properly thank you," she said with a sexy smile.

The rest of the trip was perfect. Swimming, sailing, diving, and even horseback riding on the beach.

When the week was up, they caught the same flight up to Miami. Liz upgraded Alan's seat to first class; she explained she had three hundred thousand miles and never would be able to use them all.

In Miami, Liz was connecting to San Francisco, and Alan was connecting to Dulles to meet with Robert again at CIA headquarters.

Liz gave Alan a big kiss and a hug. "I had a fantastic time. I won't even mention you saved my life."

"Thank you so much for this incredible vacation. I had a great time with you; the hotel was world class. Talk soon," Alan said before giving her a last kiss and hug. They left for their separate gates; both their flights were scheduled to depart in thirty minutes.

Liz ordered a mimosa in her first-class seat once her plane was in the air. She already missed Alan.

CHAPTER 10

GOOD NEWS AND BAD NEWS

The driver and car were waiting at Dulles, and Alan went directly to Robert's office. Eileen brought him in right away.

"Look at you—tan, smiling, and happy," Robert said as Alan sat down.

"I really had a great time. So am I hopelessly compromised?"

"Well, we have good news and bad news. What do you want first?" Robert said with a smile.

"I am a glass-half-full guy, so start with the good news."

"We have spent the last two weeks setting up the crime syndicate with the Russians and Cubans; we believe we have been very successful. We have planted information and documents that all point back to the Venezuelan crime syndicate being responsible. We covered the two groups they lost in Puerto Rico to show they were just sloppy and made mistakes that got them arrested and killed. The backroom guys have done a really good job. I don't see any cracks in the armor. We have also intercepted messages that confirm the Cubans and Russians believe they were sold out by the syndicate, and you were just a smoke screen. Their investigation of you did not find anything other than a businessman the syndicate was trying to frame to cover their tracks."

"Well, I'll have to thank the backroom guys before I leave. What is the bad news?"

"You now have a mortal enemy: the major Venezuelan crime syndicate has put a bounty of two hundred fifty thousand US dollars for your delivery to them alive. They still very much believe you are a US agent and believe if they can get you and torture you, they can get the confession they need to clear their name with the Russians and Cubans; then they will hand you over to them for their interrogation."

"Well, at least they don't have a dead bounty," Alan said with a chuckle. "So what is the plan moving forward?"

"We have decided it is time for you to perform an Absolute Resolution on the top five members of the crime syndicate. Our top man has decided he wants to let these guys know—let me quote—'they are fucking with the wrong people.' We have intel FARC is brokering a deal with the crime syndicate and the Russians and Cubans. Apparently FARC has been offered a kickback by the crime syndicate if they can get the Russians and Cubans to use them again. The backroom boys planted further documentation indicating FARC personnel were actually responsible for the loss of the last arms shipment."

"Did it work?" Alan asked.

"Appears it did. FARC executed two men for this alleged betrayal and provided proof to the Russians and Cubans. The top five syndicate guys are going to meet in Colombia with the Russians and Cubans to finalize the new deal. The meeting is to fix things to allow the crime syndicate to start smuggling larger shipments of weapons, again at one million US dollars per shipment. Our top guy wants you and a SEAL team to do the wet work for this little get-together. Let me quote: 'Rain hell on these guys.'"

"Damn, I like this."

"You're going to like it even more. You're going to be working with the same SEALs that you used to get the Cubans leading the communist FARC units last year when you were in Colombia."

"There are only five bad guys and bodyguards coming?"

"That is our intel."

"Wow. This will be the definition of raining hell. Tell the top guy this is much appreciated."

"Well, you know the big guy thinks you are Superman, but now he's pissed off, and he's throwing the kitchen sink at the syndicate. I'm glad; you are too valuable to send alone. Not that I have any doubt about the results if you went alone; El Jefe in Sinaloa could attest to that if he was still around. We have a great cover. The crime syndicate bosses will be meeting the FARC Colombians, Cubans, and possibly a Russian. The Colombian Special Forces have a reason for tracking the FARC Colombians going to the meeting; everyone else will be considered collateral damage by anyone investigating. The bonus is we will also get Cubans, and very possibly a Russian."

"Excellent. What is the ETA for these guys in Colombia?"

"They have set up the meeting for ten days from now. You need to stay on alert and continue to carry your pistol 24/7 until this is resolved."

"Roger that," Alan replied as he stood up to leave.

"You will have the package for the assignment in a couple of days. Have a good trip back; you have been upgraded to first class."

CHAPTER 11

PUERTO RICO, ON ALERT

The trip back was uneventful, and Alan spent the weekend at the office, catching up. Monday morning he sat down with Ana and went over any outstanding issues. The rest of the week was quiet and just typical office hours. After work he was now alternating his runs and bodysurfing between Isle Verde and Ocean Beach. *It will be good to get back to my beach and running in Luchetti Park after the syndicate job is completed.*

Friday morning Ana buzzed back on his telephone line. "Sonia is on the line, boss. Do you want me to pass it back to you?"

"Yes, thanks," Alan replied before hanging up and picking up the blinking line. "Alan here."

"Alan, hi. Did you enjoy your time off?" Sonia began.

"Yes, I had a good time. I got to catch up with an old friend on a yacht in the Bahamas."

"Lucky you. Listen, my friends are throwing another party in Ocean Beach tomorrow. Can you make it this time? It'll be a lot of fun."

"Sold. Sorry I missed the last one, but I would be honored to attend."

Sonia gave him the address, and they said good-bye.

Ana delivered a large package marked "CONFIDENTIAL—PRIVATE AND PERSONAL" and then closed his office door on the way out.

Alan had expected the package earlier in the week, but this was no doubt the assignment to go after the syndicate. He opened and scanned all the documents. He would have to fly out this coming Wednesday, and the action date was two days later.

Well, it is time to end this problem.

The file had photos of the top five syndicate leaders. They all appeared to be in their forties. They expected these top leaders would be traveling in an armored SUV with at least four escorts. Alan would spend the weekend working on this one.

The rest of the week was quiet, with no signs of any tails or suspicious persons. He was extra careful at the garage, the most vulnerable location where he could be found at predictable times.

Saturday morning Alan went for a run in Luchetti Park and bodysurfed at his condo for the first time in a month. All was quiet—no issues. He spent the rest of the day poring over the intel and documents and working on the intercept-and-kill plan. Having the SEALs and Black Hawk helicopters certainly made it much easier to plan the assignment.

Early evening Alan drove over to the party to meet Sonia and spent several hours there drinking a few beers and listening to music. He danced once with Sonia before saying good-bye and heading back to the condo. It was hard knowing most of the people at the party had been friends of Maria.

Back to his condo, Alan had just poured a glass of pinot when his telephone rang.

"Hello, my gladiator. How was your trip back?" Liz began.

"Great. No problems. How about you?"

"Same. No problems. I just found out we're looking at some land for a manufacturing site on the South Shore of Puerto Rico, and I'll be coming down with my boss in two weeks. Any chance you'll be around?"

"Right now it looks good. Give me your dates, and I'll try to make it happen. Are you guys staying in San Juan or on the South Shore?"

"My boss wants to play golf at Eldorado, so we'll be staying there, even though it's an hour-and-a-half drive from the proposed site," Liz said. She gave Alan the dates.

"Great hotel and excellent golf course. I'll certainly do everything I can to be on-island. Looking forward to seeing you again."

"Ditto. Missing you big time. See you in two weeks. I'll call from the airport before we take off," Liz finished before they said their good-byes.

Alan sat on the balcony watching the sunset and finishing his pinot. He had a plan; having the SEALs was a real luxury. *I'll make sure this crime-syndicate issue comes to an end.*

CHAPTER 12

BACK IN COLOMBIA

Alan was packing up his desk and getting ready to drive to the airport. Sea Secure had rescheduled an audit of the Colombian subsidiary that he had cancelled the last time he'd had a mission in Colombia.

Ana came back to his office with the preliminary information for the audit. "Here you go, boss. I have pulled the data you requested for a random review of files in Colombia. The head guy down there is very worried about the audit; he was very glad you cancelled last year. Not sure what that means."

"No one likes an outsider who doesn't know the local market to come in, review files, and second-guess decisions. I expect when I leave, he'll have a much different view of what I can bring to his process."

"Travel safe, boss. See you in a week," Ana said before closing door.

Alan called Robert, who picked up on the second ring. "Robert here."

"I'm heading to the airport and will be at the special-ops base in Colombia with the SEALs later tonight. My plan is complete, and I sent the list of equipment to the logistics guys to forward on.

That way they can work with the DOD to make sure everything is ready on site. We'll be ready to fly out in two days. FYI, I have asked for a satellite phone as a backup, and I confirmed that the DOD has air assets on the ready. The carrier *John F. Kennedy* is on exercises in the area. Need the top guy's help to confirm we can get air support if needed. We'll be in a FARC-controlled area—no good guys close. Nothing to chance on this one; got to end it, and end it for good."

"Roger that. The top guy has signed off with DOD on all your requests, and you're all set. I'll be glad to bring this saga to an end so we can get back to normal operations. We have already set up a full cover for how we found out the crime syndicate was going to be in Colombia."

"Can we trust the Colombians?"

"Yes. I feel very strongly that the level we are dealing with will not have leaks."

"Thanks, Robert. I'll be glad to call you after this one is done. Got a friend coming down the week after and will want to take three or four days off from everything, unless you have a code red."

"No problem on our end. Let the SEALs do the work on this one. Go back to being a marine recon captain and just lead," Robert said and then signed off.

Alan caught the Eastern Airlines flight and arrived in Santa Marta at about 10:00 p.m. A car delivered him to the Colombian military base in Palomino, where the SEALS were waiting at the special-operations hangar. Commander Branson and Senior Chief Rundle were waiting in the open hangar door when the car pulled up. The eight Black Hawk helicopters were sitting on the tarmac in front of the hangar, each with dual miniguns. Alan grabbed his carry-on bag from the trunk, and the CIA driver pulled off.

"Gentlemen, it's a real pleasure to see you again," Alan said as he walked over.

Commander Branson and Senior Chief Rundle both saluted, and Alan returned the salute.

"Great to be working with you again, sir," Branson said. "We have almost the exact same team members as last time. To a man, the team is looking forward to following you on this mission. We have our combat support staff guys from Intelligence, Operations, Plans and Targeting, Communications, and Air/Medical all set up to meet in the morning so you can lay out the ops plan. All of the gear you requested has arrived, and Senior Chief has completed a check of it." Branson handed Alan an olive-drab canvas case. "Here's the satellite phone you requested. The charger is already set up in your room."

"Excellent. I'm bushed and ready to turn in. Let's start at zero seven thirty tomorrow."

"You bet, sir. Follow me; I'll show you to your room," Rundle said. He grabbed Alan's carry-on and headed for the room.

"Here you go, sir, and again, great to be working with you," Rundle said as he saluted.

"Thanks, Senior Chief," Alan said. He returned the salute before closing the door. It did not take long to get to sleep.

Day 2

The SEAL planning staff was waiting after Alan finished breakfast and walked into the main conference room.

"Gentlemen, it is a real pleasure to be working with you again. Our target is expected to be a three- to four-vehicle caravan that will be traveling into Colombia from Maracaibo, Venezuela, on Highway 3 with a final destination of Riohacha, Colombia. We'll pick up the convoy with a U2 flight, so we'll have exact details on the number and type of vehicles. We are planning to set up an ambush site twelve klicks to the east of Riohacha. This is a kill mission—no prisoners."

"Do you have any other types of missions, sir?" Rundle said with a chuckle. That got a big laugh out of all.

"Good one, Senior Chief."

Alan reviewed the plans for the mission in detail. Then he turned it over to the SEAL planning staff to finish the insertion and extraction plans.

"The convoy is scheduled to be at the intercept site at zero twelve thirty tomorrow night. We'll have a new moon, so it's looking like a great setup," Alan reported as he wrapped up

"We may have some isolated showers, but that should not be a problem," the Planning and Targeting officer finished up.

Alan spent the rest of the day taking a run and playing basketball with the SEALs. There were some really good players, and there was no lack of passion to win. It was a bunch of alpha males going at it.

Alan ate dinner with Branson and Rundle, who shared some of the missions they had carried out since they last saw Alan. Alan turned in early; no telling how long tomorrow night would last.

Day 3

Alan started the morning with his usual seventy-five pushups and then just hung out in his room after breakfast. The entire team was just relaxing, as the first meeting was at 3:00 p.m. They would be loading up at 7:00 p.m. and flying to another Colombian military base in Camarones to fuel up the choppers and review any last minute intel before the strike.

Alan received the U2 report and photos at 11:30 a.m. and called a meeting with Branson, Rundle, and the planning staff.

"Here is the report and photos for your team. I did a quick review, and we have a four-vehicle convoy. Two of the SUVs are armored, and the other two are not. If we use five men per vehicle, we're probably looking at about twenty personnel. We have enough equipment to address up to six vehicles, so no issues with necessary gear. I'll leave all the final details up to you and your team, Commander. I have a satellite telephone, and we have one of our aircraft carriers on exercise nearby, USS *John F. Kennedy*. So, we've got air-support response in thirty minutes if needed. This area is controlled by FARC insurgent troops. These guys are combat hardened; many were originally trained by US troops before taking up the communist cause. We know there is a battalion-strength unit operating about twenty klicks from our insertion and ambush area."

"Thank you, sir," Commander Branson replied. "We'll finish up the final details. Meeting set for nineteen hundred, fully geared up. Lift off is at twenty hundred hours."

Alan spent the rest of the day preparing his gear: the M-14, Berettas, silencers, combat knife, and garrote. He was given a SEAL camo shirt, pants, boots, combat vest, and body armor so he would not stand out. They also fitted him with the standard SEAL helmet, night-vision goggles, and radio equipment. Alan loaded up six magazines for the M-14 and four magazines for the side-arm Beretta. He did a final last read of all the intel and reviewed the maps.

Alan walked into the hangar at 5:00 p.m., and all of the teams were already there doing final checks on each other's gear and loading all the gear onto the choppers. The flight-line crews were loading the ammunition belts for the miniguns.

He noticed almost everyone was checking out the folding-stock M-14 slung over his shoulder as he walked by. One of the chiefs could not help himself. "Sir, are you sure you don't want a real assault rifle?" he said with a big smile.

"Funny, Chief; this one works," Alan said with a chuckle as he walked over to the commander and the senior chief.

"Do you want me to do a gear check for you, sir?"

"That would be great. Thanks, Senior Chief," Alan replied.

The senior chief did the gear check. "All good, sir."

At 9:30 p.m. the teams gathered in a circle around the commander and senior chief. The senior chief gave some last-minute reminders for key timing items, the LZ, and the emergency LZ. The commander restated this was a kill mission—no prisoners. He then turned and signaled Alan.

"I already told you guys my only joke; I wanted to be a SEAL but couldn't swim." This again got a chuckle. "I want to make sure everyone is ready for this one. We had to work with some high-level Colombians, against my recommendations, to pull this off. We need to treat this mission as if we are going behind enemy lines twenty klicks outside the wire. Finally, Senior Chief, what kind of mission is this?"

"Since we are with Captain Joubert, it has got to be a kill mission," Rundle said as all the SEALs laughed.

"Let's go, guys. Time to load up," Senior Chief Rundle said as the men all began moving out to the flight line. The choppers were spooled up, hot, and ready to fly.

Within ten minutes all eight Black Hawks were in the air and flying a hundred feet above the jungle. Alan had the flashback to 'Nam he always experienced when flying over jungles at night. The Rolling Stones' "Midnight Rambler" was running through his head—the song he always played in 'Nam before recon missions. He saw the smiling faces of the two team members he had lost in 'Nam and the day he pulled their dog tags.

There was a new moon. The flight was forty-five minutes to the insertion spots after they had refueled; right on schedule, the teams roped down and took up their defensive positions. Alan could feel the surge of adrenaline. They were less than a quarter mile from the ambush zone that had been chosen. The teams waited for thirty minutes before Commander Branson gave the move-out order.

The teams quickly and quietly moved into the ambush position on Highway 3. The four teams were set up to provide a withering crossfire. The claymores were set up in the same manner as Alan had used to ambush El Jefe, only this time there were six claymores on each side, set at fifty-foot intervals. Now the hard part: waiting for the convoy.

Alan set the bezel on his watch for a thirty-minute interval, and then he sat back and rested against a tree. He was with Commander Branson and Senior Chief Rundle in Team 1, set on the left side of the road in the direction the convoy would arrive. He carefully listened, and only jungle sounds could be heard. Alan was in his typical state of alert relaxation, never understood by his 'Nam recon team, before an action. He looked down at his watch; thirty minutes had passed. Alan jumped up, startling several SEALs, and quickly moved over to Branson and Rundle.

"Commander, I believe we have a problem. The intel clearly showed at this time of night we could expect to see four passing cars in a half hour. There has not been one car. I am very concerned we had to brief the Colombian military on this operation. Something is not right."

"What do you suggest, sir?"

"I am going to get some air support off the flight deck so we have a fifteen-minute response time. Let's sit down and look at the map." Alan, the commander, and the senior chief reviewed the current position, the fallback to the primary LZ, and the emergency LZ. There was a ridge between that overlooked a clearing. This would provide the most defendable position halfway out to the primary LZ.

"Get with the teams; we have to be ready to move to the primary LZ right now, with the standard withdraw-and-cover protocol. If this is an ambush, we will immediately plan on moving to the LZ using the ridge as the *Alamo* final defense before the LZ. I don't believe the crime-syndicate convoy will be coming to this location now. I'll call in air support and act as the air coordinator while you, Commander, are directing your teams as needed. I need you to send out scouts in all four directions to see if they find anything outside the sentry positions."

Alan called the *John F. Kennedy* and gave the code to launch aircraft ready for close air support. He got confirmation that the "go fast" aircraft would be on station fifteen minutes out.

Commander Branson and Senior Chief Rundle provided a brief to all team members via radio, and the scouts were immediately deployed.

Alan again huddled with Branson and Rundle. "I was very concerned that we had to share this operation with top-level Colombian military. I got Langley to agree to one requirement. We gave the Colombians an ambush point five klicks to the east. Given the zero auto traffic now for forty-five minutes, I expect we have been set up, and the FARC units are now moving down the sides on Highway 3, having started at or near the bogus ambush point I gave them. If that is the case, one of the scouts should pick them up soon. We know the syndicate convoy was picked up right before crossing into Colombia; I expect they are going to a different location while the FARC units come after us."

"We will be ready, sir," Commander Branson immediately responded.

At that minute the radio call came in from the east scout. "We have two companies moving in, one on each side of Highway 3, from the east. These guys are heavily armed and look like real pros. I am dropping back and will stop at the sentry location. We will withdraw and help the sentries with cover fire if needed as we fall back toward the primary LZ."

"Roger that; proceed on that action," Branson radioed back.

"OK, Commander; let me know when the scout to the east meets up with the sentries. We need the claymores placed to circle north to prevent these guys from flanking in our withdrawal direction," Alan said in a calm but urgent tone.

"Roger that."

Alan pulled the satellite phone and called the *John F. Kennedy*. The combat operations officer answered immediately. "We have been compromised. We will be heading to the primary LZ for extraction. We have two FARC companies sweeping down both sides of Highway 3 from the east, heading to our position. We will need your help shortly. We have a *Little Bighorn*. Please confirm."

"Roger that; *Little Bighorn*. I confirm, *Little Bighorn*. We have twelve A6s on station. They are loaded with five-hundred-pounders and cluster bombs, and they are on station ten minutes out from your position. I'll serve as your direct link for target ID coordinates."

"Roger that."

"We have a company-sized movement coming in from the west," they heard over the radio from the scout sent west.

"We need them to set their claymores to the west as well. Let me know where they are set, as I'll use that as the drop point for the air strike when they start going off," Alan advised Branson.

"Roger that," Branson said, and he began providing instructions over the radio.

Alan immediately began plotting the coordinates for the air strikes.

"Choppers are thirty minutes out. This is going to be really tight," Branson advised Alan.

"Confirm the claymores are set. We are going to be in a gunfight on the way out. I'll also control the choppers with the miniguns so we have coordination with the go-fast boys."

"Roger that; I'll work with the senior chief on the withdrawal plan with the teams. All claymores to the east and west have been set with trip wires. I have the sentries pulling back as soon as they first pick up movement."

"Roger that; I'll be calling in the air strikes right after the claymores go off at those coordinates," Alan responded. He called the carrier operations officer on the satellite telephone to advise the estimated strike time in ten minutes. The lead chopper pilot called in to Branson and advised fifteen minutes out from the LZ.

Branson advised the chopper pilot that Alan was coordinating all air strikes for both carrier aircraft and chopper mini-gun runs.

In another five minutes, the claymores in the east began to go off, each with the seven hundred one-eighth-inch steel balls powered by C4. Alan confirmed the coordinates to the east with the carrier operations officer, and within minutes they could hear the A6 intruders beginning their low-level runs to the east. The five-hundred-pounders and cluster bombs carpeted the jungle to the east with explosions. At the same moment, the claymores to the west began to go off. Alan confirmed the west coordinates and ordered this strike. The claymores were closer, and the A6 intruders began their low-level runs west, passing right over the SEALs' position. Again the jungle was rocked with explosions as the five-hundred-pounders and cluster bombs began to go off.

Teams Three and Four set up defensive positions, led by Senior Chief Rundle, and released multiple gray smoke grenades. Teams One and Two, with Branson and Alan, began to withdraw to the ridge defense position to the north. Teams One and Two left their six M72 LAWs with Teams Three and Four. The withdrawing teams could hear heavy fire coming from the SEALs' defensive positions behind them.

"We have at least a FARC company-strength attack, and we are in direct contact and firefight. Withdrawal will be very difficult, as they are starting to flank us both left and right," Senior Chief Rundle radioed.

Alan ran over to Branson. "We've got to go back. They are going to need every one of us to get out. We will have to do a combined defend-and-retreat action together to protect their flanks."

"Roger that, sir. As a CIA operative, you should go to the LZ."

"No way, Commander. Let's go."

"Roger that. Teams One and Two, we are going back to support the flanks and withdraw together," Branson radioed as both teams and Alan started back at a full run.

At that very moment, Rundle called, "Team Four, man down, KIA."

When teams One and Two arrived, a massive firefight was in progress. Teams One and Two and Alan immediately began to stop the FARC units flanking Teams Three and Four. The SEALs' night vision and muzzle-flash suppressors provide a significant advantage in this night firefight. Alan was on Branson's shoulder. Alan had already picked off five FARC troops when Branson was hit in the neck. The round had hit his right carotid artery. Alan pulled a compression pad from his side pant's pocket applying full pressure. "Stay with me Branson, stay with me," Alan shouted over the gunfire but Commander Branson was gone in a minute.

Seconds later a call came over the radio, "Man down, Team Three. Medic needed."

This was one of the most intense firefights Alan had ever experienced. RPGs were hitting all around them. They were heavily out-gunned, with the odds five to one against them.

"Commander Branson is KIA," Alan radioed out to Rundle.

"Sir, you are now in command. We will continue to withdraw and defend," Rundle quickly responded.

"Roger that. In about one hundred fifty yards, there is an opening in the jungle and the *Alamo* ridge behind it. This will allow me to call in a very close air strike and the choppers with the miniguns. Have the teams withdraw around the open area and stop one hundred yards behind it on the ridge top. Mark the open space with infrared strobes. I'll be calling in the go-fast boys and the choppers to hit them at that point," Alan said. He picked up Branson in a buddy carry and began moving back, with team members providing cover.

All the teams began moving back quickly, using gray smoke grenades as cover. They approached the open area, with Teams One and Two heading around the right side and Teams Three and Four the left side. Team members on both sides dropped infrared strobes for target marking on both sides of the opening. When they were over a hundred yards past the opening up on the ridge, Alan called the air controller to advise of infrared strobes for the target markers and their *Alamo* defensive location on the ridge. The A6 intruders roared in first and dropped five-hundred-pounders and cluster bombs. They were followed by two choppers that emptied their miniguns into the target areas. The open area with the infrared strobes was an excellent target locator.

The gunfire from the FARC units was now significantly diminished and allowed an orderly withdrawal back to the LZ, with the cover defense holding the hilltop. Alan had the last two choppers again make runs with their miniguns back seventy-five yards from the ridge to catch the FARC troops leaving cover and just starting to move again.

Teams Three and Four set up defensive positions at the LZ, and Teams One and Two loaded into two choppers and were off. Rundle, with Teams Three and Four, loaded out as the last two choppers emptied their miniguns on the FARC troopers trying to advance on the LZ. The last two teams were off on two choppers, taking heavy ground fire on the way out.

"We got one Team-Three member hit on chopper four; he is under medical attention," Senior Chief Rundle reported.

Alan sat quietly in the chopper, looking at Branson lying against the side wall. *Fucking corrupt Colombians; I knew it was a fucking mistake to work with them. There are some really good men who paid the ultimate price for this FUBAR by the State Department and DOD working with the crooked Colombians. Thank heavens I gave the Colombians the wrong ambush spot, or we would all be dead.*

The choppers landed at the flight line, and the support crew offloaded the two dead and two wounded SEALs. Alan pulled his magazine from his M14 and ejected the chambered round. He had only two rounds left in his last magazine. Rundle walked over to Alan and gave him a crisp salute.

"Thank you, sir. We would all be dead without you."

"Senior Chief, your men did an outstanding job. We are all alive because you guys are the best of the best."

"Sir, do you want to attend the post-action meeting?" Rundle said very carefully.

"No, Senior Chief, but I do want to talk to the men before I call Langley."

The SEALs had grouped in the hangar as Alan came walking over. "Gentlemen, I can only say that was an outstanding response to a dire situation. You all performed outstandingly. It was an honor to fight alongside you. We lost two great men, who made the ultimate sacrifice. I stand here to honor them. Thank you."

Every SEAL immediately saluted, and Senior Chief Rundle called out, "Sir, thank you again for saving our asses." Alan crisply returned the salute and headed off to his private room.

Alan stripped off his gear and clothing, which were impregnated with cordite and blood from carrying Commander Branson. *Branson was only two feet away. Why him and not me?* Alan jumped into the shower and scrubbed himself clean.

He dried off and wrapped the towel around his waist before dialing Langley. Robert answered on the first ring, "Alan, are you OK?"

"I am fucking fine, but we brought back two dead—one was Commander Branson—and two severely wounded."

"Damn, I am so sorry Alan," Robert quietly responded.

"The fucking Colombians gave us up. If I had not noticed the lack of highway traffic, or given the Colombians the incorrect ambush location, or if there had not been a carrier on exercise nearby, we would all be dead. We were up against a planned battalion-strength attack—caught in the middle. You tell those guys at the State Department to go fuck themselves, and I'll never be part of any action if we share intel with anyone outside the company or the DOD."

"Understood. FYI, our top guy went straight to POTUS on this one. POTUS is currently raining on the State Department parade."

"That doesn't help Commander Branson or Chief Wilson or the two guys in ICU."

"I know, Alan. I know. Everyone knows you didn't want the mission cleared with the Colombians. Believe me; you are very much on record. The loss of these two men and the two in ICU will not be forgotten. The crime syndicate will pay."

"What about the fucking Colombians? I'll call you when I get back to Puerto Rico. I only hope the crime-syndicate boys send another team, as I'll personally handle them. I want a plan to eliminate the top syndicate guys who got away; I want to be part of any action."

"Understood. Call me tomorrow when you get to the office."

Alan cancelled the audit. No way could he handle that right now.

The trip back was uneventful. It was a two-Bloody-Mary morning.

CHAPTER 13

WINDING DOWN FROM A FIREFIGHT

Alan made it back to his condo at 7:30 p.m. and grabbed a Corona beer out of the refrigerator. He sat down on a chair on the balcony. *Damn, Branson was a fine man, and so was Wilson, besides both being top-notch SEALs. Why Branson and not me? I was right next to him.*

Alan had gone through these same reoccurring feelings in the past, but this time it was different. Every day in 'Nam had felt like it might be the last; this was a mission that should have been a simple in and out. *Fucking corrupt Colombians!*

He continued to sit quietly, thinking of Branson's family: his wife, four-year-old girl, and six-year-old boy. *I'll fly back for the service.*

Alan slept very fitfully, waking several times from dreams of the firefight and Commander Branson.

The next morning Alan called Robert.

"Any news on the two wounded SEALs?" Alan began.

"Yes. They are both going to be OK and are out of ICU. Senior Chief Rundle has sent his action report to the DOD, and the top guy already has a copy. Your new nickname at Langley is The Legend. That was truly an amazing exhibition of on-the-run planning and execution. We are getting reports from the Colombians that you and the SEALs decimated a top-notch battle-hardened FARC battalion. Reportedly over two hundred twenty killed and another hundred wounded. The top guy wants to give you another award that you will never be able to talk about or show to anybody."

"I want to attend the service for Commander Branson and Chief Wilson. Let me know where and when as soon as you can."

"I knew you would; you need to fly up tomorrow—it's the following day at ten hundred hours."

"Have logistics book me a ticket. You and I also have to sit down and decide exactly how we are going to take care of the leaders of the crime syndicate. I also will be very interested to hear the chatter and intel the backroom guys have come up with since the firefight."

"Roger that. I'll also be attending the services with you. I'll pick you up at the hotel at zero nine thirty and drive us to the service. I can then drive you back to Langley, and we can go over the intel. What was it like to be back in a full-blown firefight?"

"I never stopped to think; it was all just pure reaction based on my recon work in the past and adrenaline. That was one epic nighttime firefight. I had three rounds left for my M14: one in the chamber and two in my last magazine. I would have been down to a Berretta pistol after that."

"Holy smoke, that was cutting it close. OK, Legend. See you in a couple of days."

Alan flew out the next morning and then took a cab over to the hotel. His pager went off, and it was Ana from his office. When he got to his room, he called her.

"What's up?"

"You got a call from Liz, and she left a callback number. You also have an appointment for Monday afternoon with another pissed-off broker and his client. I'll leave the details on your desk," Ana reported.

Alan called Liz right after.

"Liz," she said after answering on the third ring.

"Hey, Liz. Hope all is well."

"Alan, I'm so glad to hear from you. I wanted to confirm you will be around next Wednesday when I get to Puerto Rico."

"Yes, sure will. I'm looking forward to seeing you again."

"I am too; can't wait. We are overnighting in Miami and will arrive in Puerto Rico at 2:30 p.m. We are off until the next day. My boss has scheduled a round of golf for the afternoon we arrive, and I'll be free while he plays."

"Great. I'll pick you up at the Eldorado Hotel. We can bodysurf at the beach at my condo, and I'll barbecue."

"Excellent. You have a date," she said.

Alan went to dinner and then to have a drink in the bar. Two marines in uniform were sitting at the bar quietly talking. One of the marines was about Alan's age, and the other was older: a major and a gunnery sergeant. They both had 'Nam ribbons and Combat Infantry Badges. Alan sat down and ordered a Dewar's scotch on the rocks. After finishing the drink, he called the bartender over and quietly said, "Give me a check, and give those two guys a drink on me—whatever they are drinking."

"Will do; I'll let them know."

"No, don't bother them; wait until I've left. Just tell them it is from a Third Battalion recon brother."

"Will do; I get that a lot here."

The next morning Robert picked Alan up in front of the hotel, and they drove to Arlington. They were both quiet. Alan was in a black suit, white shirt, and black tie with gray fleur-de-lis prints. Robert was also in a black suit, white shirt, and black tie.

The ceremony was so very solemn on a bright, sunny day. Commander Branson's wife was beautiful and brave. So were his kids. Chief Wilson's mother was there to accept his flag. All of the SEALs from the mission were present. After the service Alan gave his condolences to Branson's wife and Wilson's mother. Then Alan walked over to Senior Chief Rundle. "Senior Chief, hope you and the guys are OK."

"We are, sir. Again, thank you for getting the rest of us home."

"You all got yourselves home; I was along for the ride."

"Take care of yourself, sir. We would be honored to work with you again."

"Same here, Senior Chief. Give my best to all the guys."

Alan and Robert left after the two twenty-one-gun salutes and the presentation of the flags to Mrs. Branson and Mrs. Wilson.

On the way back, Alan sat quietly for a while. Finally, he looked at Robert and asked, "Do you have a plan?"

"Working on one. The backroom boys have a great deal of new intel. The top guy wants to, quote, 'crush the crime syndicate; forget the rules.'"

At Langley, Robert brought Alan into his office and told Eileen no interruptions unless there was a code red. Robert and Alan sat at the small conference table in the corner of his office.

"Alan, I know how tough today was for you. I could see it in your eyes."

"This never should have happened. A Colombian traded money for the lives of two outstanding men and put many more in harm's way. Yes, it makes me sick."

"Let me go over what the backroom boys have discovered since the firefight. To start, the Colombians have gone public that this action was between one of their top special-operations units, defeating overwhelming odds with some timely assistance from a US Navy aircraft carrier on exercise to help defend democracy in Colombia and other South America countries. The reported body count for FARC was two hundred and twenty-one killed and over one hundred wounded. This, of course, is great propaganda for the Colombians, who have had nothing but setbacks in all their recent encounters with FARC."

"I guess this raises the question: did we get used for this very purpose?"

"POTUS and our backroom boys asked the same question."

"What intel do they have on the Russians' and Cubans' take on this incident?"

"This is where it gets complicated. The Russians, Cubans, and crime syndicate were told by FARC that the planned meeting had been discovered and needed to be cancelled. FARC advised they were going to counter-ambush the Colombia Special Forces that were going to ambush the meeting. This would point to the high probability the Colombian government or military leaked that the meeting ambush was going to be carried out by their own special forces. The crime-syndicate convoy was only a decoy to assure you guys were inserted. The Russians' and Cubans' chatter shows they clearly believe this was Colombian Special Forces aided by US carrier-based aircraft. To make a long story short, it appears you are still clear with the Russians and Cubans and still carry a bounty with the Venezuelan crime syndicate. Only one change: your bounty alive by the syndicate is now three hundred fifty thousand US dollars."

"Well, at least it is still a live bounty," Alan said with a smile. "The FARC battalion commander had to know they were not up against Colombian Special Forces."

"You left nothing behind to prove it wasn't the Colombia special-ops guys. The Colombians went to great lengths to prove it was their men. There is TV footage of two of their men leaving the hospital in their special-ops uniforms with ski masks and bandages. The Colombians then held a big televised ceremony and presented medals to the whole Special Forces unit for their outstanding valor. They talked about killing many FARC troops. The story and video have been all over the news. There were also front-page articles in all the Colombian newspapers with photos of these two guys."

Alan shook his head in disgust. "Wow, this is crazy. The fucking Colombian government sent us into this trap and cost the lives of two outstanding men for propaganda purposes? Why did they believe we would have a chance in this surprise ambush?"

"We had some fog of war on our side. The Colombians contacted us to say they were concerned about an ambush right before you figured it out. We relayed this to the carrier operations officer, but you had just ordered them to launch ground-support aircraft, so he assumed you already knew. I think the Colombians had no idea they would come after you guys with a battalion. Still, there are many questions to be answered. We're still not sure we have it all right yet. Regardless, there are some very embarrassed people at the State Department. I'll send you the final company action summary when it's complete."

"OK. Let's get back to 'crushing the top guys of the crime syndicate; forget the rules.'"

"You bet. We'll have a plan by next week. In the meantime, you can go back to Puerto Rico and enjoy some time off until the top guy signs off on the plan. Do you want surveillance and backup? The top guy said no limit in protecting you until this syndicate issue is resolved."

"I'll take you up on surveillance and backup. I really do not want to be running solo while I have a guest; it's not fair to her."

"You got it; we will have the personnel start the surveillance at the airport when you land tomorrow. Let's see if you can identify our surveillance guys," Robert closed with a chuckle.

CHAPTER 14

R&R

The trip back to Puerto Rico was uneventful. Alan was on full alert to pick up his surveillance. He threw his carry-on bag into his trunk and started out for his condo. It took Alan twenty minutes before he picked up the tail surveillance car that he knew was there. The guy was good; excellent spy-craft work. That would certainly help take the pressure off this coming week.

Alan called Liz when he got back to his condo.

"Liz here."

"Hi, Liz. I'm back in Puerto Rico and just wanted to follow up and make sure your schedule is still good for Wednesday."

"Glad you called; I was just getting ready to call you. I spoke to my boss, and I can meet you at the airport and spend the night, if that works for you. I have to be ready for the car to pick me up at ten Thursday morning to drive with my boss to the South Shore."

"That works fine; I'll plan on meeting you at the gate."

"Great. Can't wait to see you again," Liz said before they said their good-byes.

On Monday Alan handled the pissed-off broker and caught up on paperwork. At the end of the day, Ana came to his office door. "Boss, can I have a private word with you?"

"Sure. Come in, close the door, and sit down."

"I'm worried about you. You don't seem to be yourself. Are you OK?"

"I'm fine. Thank you for your concern. I found out over the weekend I lost some close friends."

"Oh, I am so sorry to hear that. Is there anything I can do?"

"No, thank you. I am going to take off Wednesday and will be back in the office on Monday. Hold the fort. If there's a really important issue, you can page me."

"Don't worry. We'll handle everything until Monday," Ana replied before going over and hugging Alan.

"Thank you, Ana. You are the best."

Alan could spot both the woman tailing him and the man dressed in a jogging suit that was his backup when he left the office on the way to the parking garage. Both gave Alan a slight head nod when they saw he had identified them.

Tuesday was quiet at work; Alan packed up to leave and now was getting used to his tail and backup.

On Wednesday Alan was waiting by the gate to meet Liz when her American Airlines flight arrived. She and her boss were in first class, so they were the second people off the aircraft. Liz looked stunning in a dark charcoal suit, white blouse, straight skirt that fell slightly above her knees and fit her like a glove, and red high-heeled shoes. Her hair was pinned up on her head, and she looked very businesslike as well as elegant. Her boss was in his midfifties, in good shape, and was about five foot ten inches tall. He was dressed in an expensive Savile Row suit. Liz saw Alan immediately and came running over to kiss and hug him. Liz's boss looked Alan over carefully. Alan was dressed in a white Guevara shirt, striped shorts, and flip-flops.

"John, I want to introduce you to Alan. Alan, John is my boss," Liz said after she let go of Alan.

"You guys have a good time," John said. "See you tomorrow, Liz. We'll pick you up at the address you gave me at ten tomorrow morning."

"I'm so happy this work trip came up," Liz told Alan. "I was dancing in my office hoping I would be able to see you."

"Great to see you too. You're quite elegant with your hair up," Alan said.

"Well, I certainly plan to let my hair down with you," she said with a laugh and a sexy smile.

"Let's go to my condo. We have time to go to the beach and then I'll barbecue."

The rest of the afternoon was excellent. Liz wore a white string bikini, and she was in perfect shape. She had every man watching her any time she got up or went in the water. Her blond hair was down to her waist before she put it in a ponytail.

At 5:30 p.m. they went back to the condo. Both showered, and Liz came out in the terrycloth robe Alan had given her. Alan was in a T-shirt and shorts.

Liz put her arms around Alan, kissed him, and pulled him back to the bedroom. An hour and a half later, they lay breathless next to each other.

"I have never been with anyone like you, Alan," Liz whispered.

"You are quite an athlete," he said with a chuckle.

They both showered again, and Alan opened the pinot, turned on the jazz, and prepared to light the BBQ. They sat on the balcony, and Liz told Alan about growing up in Marin County and then attending Yale for undergraduate and graduate school. She had played soccer at Yale; that certainly explained her athletic build and great legs. When she finished relating how she had been recruited for her current job, she sat back and quietly waited for Alan.

"You have certainly been on the fast track, and I can only say well done," he said.

"Tell me about you. I know nothing about you other than I never want to make you mad," she said with a smile.

"Not much to tell. Worked as a captain in the oil patch and then went to work as a marine consultant. Here I am. I'm lucky to have been given the assignment to manage the Caribbean and Central and South America for Sea Secure. I grew up in New Orleans, and as you know, I'm a personal friend of the Neville Brothers, and I can dance," he said with a chuckle.

Liz could not help laughing and immediately leaned over and wrapped her arms around Alan. "You left out that you should be competing in the Olympics for sex," she said as she dragged him back to the bedroom. "We can eat later."

The next morning they were up at 8:30 a.m., a very late morning for Alan. He fixed Manhattan omelets using the famous recipe of the Camellia Grill in New Orleans.

"Well, damn. On top of everything else, you can barbecue and cook," Liz said as she finished up her breakfast. "We should be back from the South Shore at seven thirty this evening. Can I buy you dinner at the El Capitán, el capitán?"

"Sure. Call me when you guys are leaving the South Shore, and I can meet you there."

The car picked Liz up right on schedule. Before she left, Liz wrapped her arms around Alan and gave him a deep, lingering kiss.

"Good luck today. Hope all goes well," Alan said as he held the door. The driver took her hanging bag and stored it in the trunk. Alan could see John giving him a less-than-friendly look.

"See you tonight," Liz said to Alan before he closed the door. The Mercedes took off quickly once the door was closed.

Alan called Robert as soon as he got back to the condo.

"Just wanted to check in to see how the plans were going."

"For the record, I have already heard from the surveillance and backup teams, and I understand you picked them up right away."

"They are very good; I feel very comfortable having a guest visiting."

"Great. We're going through every option. We will have a decision from the top guy next week. Legend, I am proud to advise you that you have been awarded the Distinguished Intelligence Cross for your work in Colombia. The award reads, 'Voluntary acts of extraordinary heroism involving the acceptance of existing dangers with conspicuous fortitude and exemplary courage.' You have now received the DIC and the Intelligence Star you got last year for Paraguay; we have nothing else to give you. Of course, you can't show or tell anyone about this latest award."

"I hope Commander Branson and Chief Wilson are receiving posthumous awards as well."

"They are. Branson and Wilson have been awarded Navy Crosses, and all the SEALs will be receiving Bronze Stars, with Purple Hearts, of course, for the two wounded. They are both doing great and out of the hospital."

"I'm glad to hear that; they all certainly deserve those medals."

"I'll call you next week as soon as the decision is made."

"Roger that," Alan closed before signing off.

Liz called at 4:30 p.m. and advised she would back at the Eldorado at 6:30 p.m., so dinner at 7:30 p.m. would work great.

Alan was right on time at the Eldorado, and he called up to Liz's room.

"I'll meet you in the lobby. We have a reservation at El Capitán for dinner."

"Great. I have my car in front," Alan replied.

Alan spotted Liz as soon as the elevator door opened, as did every other man in the lobby. She was wearing a white strapless sundress that fell just above her knees and high-heeled wedge shoes. She was tanned, athletic, and stunningly beautiful. She quickly walked over, wrapped her arms around his neck, and gave him a long kiss.

"So how do I look?" she said, smiling.

"I was speechless. You look absolutely stunning."

Dinner at El Capitán was superb. Liz ordered an excellent bottle of expensive French champagne to start; they both had oysters as appetizers and lobster for the main course, with another excellent bottle of French white wine.

"How was your day?" Alan asked as he finished his lobster.

"Very good. Today was just a very preliminary look and to hear about incentives from the government. It's looking promising. It would be wonderful to have a reason to come to Puerto Rico on a regular basis," she said with her sly, sexy look.

"Great. How is the rest of your schedule?"

"John has invited us both to a round of golf tomorrow. He said the course is outstanding. What do you think?"

"Haven't played golf in a while. What do you want to do?"

"Once we play golf, I'm off duty and free until I fly out Sunday afternoon. I think my boss would appreciate me playing, and I insisted you be invited. Just a heads-up: he's married with two kids but has tried to come on to me several times when we travel."

"So that's why I got 'the look.'"

"Yes, I saw that too."

"Well, hell, let's play some golf. I'll rent shoes and clubs rather than going back for mine tomorrow."

Liz insisted on picking up the tab, and they had a great night in her suite.

The tee time was at 10:00 a.m. Liz looked simply amazing in a golf skirt and polo shirt with her long blond hair gathered up in a ponytail beneath a visor. John insisted on paying for Alan's rental clubs and golf shoes. Liz had a big smile when Alan asked for size thirteen golf shoes. When he asked for an extra-large left-handed golf glove, Liz could not help chuckling.

There was definite tension, but the golf was great. John insisted Liz ride in his cart. Alan shot 85, John shot 93, and Liz shot a solid 98. Alan's putting skills carried the day. He made several puts over fifteen feet. John had insisted on betting and lost $300. Alan tried to not accept payment, but John would not hear it. They had beers after; Alan and John ended the day cordially.

"See you at the office on Monday, Liz," John said as he got up to leave them.

"Thank you so much for the round of golf. See you Monday."

Alan thanked John for the round of golf, and they firmly shook hands before he left.

"Well, that was interesting," Alan said. "He sure can't keep his eyes off of you—not that I blame him. Sorry I won." He chuckled.

"No, you aren't; you won in more ways than one. John needs to lose every once in a while; believe me—it doesn't happen often."

The rest of the weekend was amazing. They bodysurfed and barbecued, and Alan taught Liz how to salsa; she really knew how to move. Alan drove her to the airport on Sunday afternoon and walked her to the gate.

"Well, I may have officially fallen for you," she said with a weak smile.

"I had a wonderful time with you, Liz, and look forward to seeing you again." Alan paused as decided how much to tell Liz. "I want you to know I lost my fiancée last year...I'm still struggling."

Liz grabbed both sides of his face and kissed him. She continued holding his face a few inches away, looking directly into his eyes. "I am here for you. I knew there was something; I'll be here and will wait as long as I have to for you to heal," she said. She kissed him again with a tear in her eye before turning to board the aircraft.

Alan watched her, now knowing this "no strings attached" was not going to work for Liz.

CHAPTER 15

NO GRENADA VACATION

Alan's pager buzzed on the drive home from dropping Liz off. He called Robert as soon as he got to his condo.

"The invasion of Grenada is a go for this coming Friday. The top guy has decided he does not want you on the ground for this one. Too many moving parts. Off the record, he believes the operation is being thrown together too quickly without a good command structure. We haven't done anything like this since 'Nam. The DOD intel guys want you to fly out to the USS *Guam,* the flagship for the Amphibious Readiness Group for the invasion. They're going to send a Sea Stallion chopper as soon as they're in range of San Juan with an ETA of Tuesday at zero seven hundred. They want you to brief the SEALs who are going in early for recon and disruption and to rescue Governor General Scoon."

"Damn. I want to go on this one."

"I know; I tried to get the top guy to reconsider, even though I agree with him. I know you wanted to go back. He did not want to even discuss it; he shut me down immediately."

"OK. Where am I catching the chopper?"

"The coast guard airfield."

"Roger that. Tuesday at zero seven hundred at the coast guard air station," Alan acknowledged before they signed off.

Alan sat looking out his balcony window. *Damn. I really want to go back with the SEALs.*

Monday when Alan got to the office, he began to go through the stack of issues and files Ana had left for him. By the time Ana got in, he had finished prioritizing. Ana popped her head in the door. "Hope you had a good time."

"I had a great time. Thanks, Ana. I'll have to take off a few more days starting Tuesday. Keep up the great work; I know you will take care. I'll not be able to get pages while I am gone."

"No problem, boss. We'll take care of everything."

On Tuesday Alan was at the gate of the coast guard air station at 6:30 a.m. He drove to the chopper tarmac and parked. A commander came walking over as he got out of the car. "Mr. Joubert?"

"Yes."

"I'm Commander Phillips. We are expecting you. We just got a call from the Sea Stallion, and they have an ETA of zero seven fifteen. Chopper is running a bit late. We have a flight suit for you, sir."

Alan followed the commander into the locker room, changed into a coast guard chopper-pilot flight suit, and hung his clothes in the locker.

The Sea Stallion arrived exactly at 7:15 a.m. A crew member got out and jogged over to the commander and Alan.

Alan jogged back with him, and they both jumped in the chopper, which was ready to fly. He took a seat in the passenger compartment, and the crewman handed him a set of earphones.

"Glad to have you on board, sir. We have an hour-and-a-half flight, so sit back and relax," the pilot advised as they lifted off.

The flight out was smooth and right on schedule. Alan could see the fleet on the horizon. The carrier *Independence* and the flagship *Guam* were in the center of the formation. The chopper settled on the *Guam,* and the crew member exited and advised Alan to embark.

A marine captain was waiting to take Alan below. He led Alan directly to the operations center. The ops center personnel were busy laying out the complex operation on clear board maps and a large electronic table map.

The captain brought Alan over to a full colonel.

"Mr. Joubert, it's a pleasure to meet you," the colonel said. "We all got to read your outstanding recon report from earlier in the year. Much appreciated. We'll have a few questions, but you're here because the SEAL teams that are going in early made the request. I understand you have worked with some of the teams in the past. The captain will bring you to their ops center now, and we will take a short amount of your time after you finish that work."

"Thank you, sir," Alan said. He followed the captain to the SEAL ops center, where he spotted Senior Chief Rundle right away. Rundle immediately came over with a commander at his side.

"Captain Joubert, sir, I want you to meet our new commander, Mike Welsch."

"Pleasure to meet you, Commander."

"I can assure you I'm honored to meet you. The team gave me a full brief, and I read the action report; I was in awe. I also heard you carried Branson, my good friend, all the way back to the LZ. Once we found out you had completed the recon report, the entire team asked to have you fly out so we could meet with you for questions and planning. We have our combat support staff guys from Intelligence, Operations, Plans and Targeting, Communications, and Air/Medical all set up to meet with you. The other SEAL team commander, both senior chiefs, and I'll attend. We'll be asking you to clarify parts of your report as well as your thoughts on how best to carry out our missions based on your time on the ground."

"I am honored, Commander. I'll be glad to provide my two cents."

The commander led Rundle and Alan into a side planning room, where all the SEALs were already waiting. When they walked in, every SEAL got up and saluted Alan. Alan crisply responded. Over the next five hours, he answered all their questions and provided his ideas for how to best complete the missions. They all listened very carefully and took notes on his comments, issues, and recommendations. Finally, they all sat back and reviewed their notes to see if there were any other items.

Commander Welsch stood up. "Anything else before we let Mr. Joubert meet with the senior staff?"

Senior Chief Rundle stood up and smiled. "Is Captain Joubert going with us?"

"I requested to go, but my boss's boss said no. I want all of you to know that if I had a choice right now, I would be ready to go," Alan responded quietly.

"You certainly would be welcome, sir, but you would have to take off that coast guard flight suit," Rundle responded with a big chuckle. All the SEALs got a good laugh.

Alan pushed back to leave, and every SEAL in the room stood up at attention and saluted him. "Godspeed," Alan said as he crisply saluted and headed back to the main ops center.

Interestingly, the senior staff had only a very few questions. They thanked Alan for taking the time to fly out and told him they had arranged a chopper back.

The captain led Alan back out to the chopper. "Senior staff spends fifteen minutes with you, and the SEALs spend five hours. I fear this is being rushed; we haven't done anything like this since Vietnam."

"Godspeed," Alan said before he ran out to the Sea Stallion chopper that was spooled up and ready to fly. The trip back was uneventful. Alan sat wishing he could be going with the SEALs. *I certainly hope this rush to invasion is not a FUBAR.*

CHAPTER 16

DOMINICAN REPUBLIC AND FUBAR

Alan was in the office the next morning, and all was quiet. He got a new urgent request from Sea Secure New York. An interisland container ship had capsized at the dock while loading containers in Puerto Plata, Dominican Republic. Sea Secure had fifteen customers with containers on board. The assignment was to determine why the vessel had capsized and the condition of the containers and cargo. He would be met at the airport by a colonel of the Dominican Republic Army, who would attend with him. There had been multiple losses of life, both ship's crew and longshoremen who had been loading the ship at the time of the accident.

The Prinair flight was right on schedule, and the colonel was waiting for him at immigration and customs. Alan was cleared right away and got in the colonel's car to head for Puerto Plata.

"Please to meet you, Mr. Joubert. I am Colonel Gomez. I understand you are an expert and will be able to help us determine the cause of this tragedy."

"Colonel, I am of course representing my client Sea Secure, which has insureds with cargo on the vessel. I'll ask if I can share with you."

"Excellent. I look forward to hearing from you tomorrow morning after you have finished your work today."

The colonel lead Alan out to his Mercedes and the driver opened the door for the colonel and Alan got in the other back door. During the first thirty minutes of the drive, Alan noticed four rusted and abandoned Dodge K-cars on the side of the road. "Colonel, I have noticed several abandoned Dodge K-cars along the side of the road."

"Yes, some guy from Puerto Rico brought these cars here and sold them very cheaply. I bought one for my wife. They have all stopped working and are useless. That guy had better never come back to DR."

Damn, these have got to be the flooded cars I salvaged off of Culebra. I'll have to talk to Miguel and find out who he sold them to. Thank heavens the colonel doesn't know he's sitting next to the guy who pulled them out of the saltwater.

They reached the dock, and the sight was surreal. The 350-foot container ship was lying on the port side next to the dock, half under water. The gangway was still down on the starboard side, and containers were still floating near the ship. Five longshoremen and two deckhands had been killed. A container of chicken parts had been destroyed, and the chicken parts had brought a large number of sharks into the harbor. The scene was chaotic.

Alan took photos and then, working through the colonel, was able to interview both the captain and chief engineer of the vessel, both of whom were being held by the harbor police. In a very short time, the cause of capsize became apparent to Alan. The chief engineer had been transferring fuel and ballast at the time of the incident. The vessel had been low on fuel oil as well. The stability of the fully loaded container ship had been compromised due to the lack of sufficient fuel oil and ballast. After five hours, the colonel drove Alan back to the Sheraton Hotel. Alan promised the colonel that he would check on sharing his findings in the morning.

Alan sent a telex to Sea Secure requesting permission to release his findings to the colonel and turned in for the night.

The next morning Alan was up early, and his telephone message light was blinking. He called and was told he had a telex at the front desk. Alan checked out and picked up the telex. Sea Secure did not want him to share his report.

The colonel was waiting outside the hotel on schedule to take Alan back to the airport. Alan explained he was instructed not to share his report but gave the colonel an off-the-record account of the cause of the incident. The colonel was very thankful and promised he would not say he got it from Alan. When Alan reached the airport, the colonel thanked him again and gave him a business card in case he ever came back.

When Alan landed, his pager immediately went off four times. One page was from Ana, and three were from Robert. Alan immediately went to a payphone and called Robert.

"Robert here."

"I was in Dominican Republic on a Sea Secure assignment. What's up?"

"I have some real bad news. The SEALs were sent in yesterday, two days before the invasion. It was 'damn the torpedoes; full speed ahead' on the invasion despite a force-seven storm. They were airdropped in the sea, along with their inflatables. Four drowned, and the rest barely escaped a patrol boat when the motor of one of their inflatables flooded. The mission was aborted, and they rescued the survivors after having to sink the patrol boat. They have sent a second SEAL team today, believe it or not, but they were overcome by the weather and rescued without injury or causalities. This was Rundle and his team. The top guy was certainly right on this one. Glad you weren't there."

"What an absolute FUBAR and SNAFU. What a sad waste of some top-notch men. Who the hell authorized this action in those weather conditions? I expect they have lost any element of surprise they may have had."

"The go order came from the very top," Robert replied sadly.

"Roger that. When is the full-scale invasion?"

"Tomorrow; I'll keep you up to speed."

"Any news on the plans for the crime-syndicate top guys?"

"It's still in the works. Believe me, it's not on a back burner. I met with the top guy for an hour yesterday. We are truly looking at everything. The top guy has authorized your surveillance and backup to remain in place until this is resolved. He wants this to be the last time we have to deal with this problem. Stay tuned."

"Roger that; pass on my thanks to the top guy. It's great to not have to be on full-action alert all the time," Alan said and then signed off.

CHAPTER 17

THE MAN HAS A PLAN

Alan took it easy over the weekend, watching the TV news and reading the newspapers. By Sunday the fighting was over, and Grenada was secured. Robert gave him updates. On the third day there had been a friendly fire incident where an A7 struck a Second Brigade command post, with seventeen wounded and one dead. Actual combat deaths in action were few. The SEALs got trapped trying to free Governor General Scoon, but AC-130 gunships, A7 Corsairs, and Cobra attack choppers held off the attackers for twenty-four hours until a company from Twenty-Second Marine Assault reached them.

Alan was in the office as usual on Monday and called Robert immediately.

"Robert here."

"I have been reading the news. Sounds like the top guy was right. This operation sounds like it left a great deal to be desired."

"They learned a great deal. The primary problem was the lack of a fully integrated command structure. We're lucky we weren't up against a more formidable force."

"Rather be lucky than good."

"I'll need you to come up next week. We will have the plan for the syndicate guys, and you will also want to attend the opening ceremony for the Vietnam Memorial. Of course, you can't wear your dress uniform and military decorations."

"Can you share anything on the plan now?"

"No, I need to wait. The plan is in process, and I don't want to discuss it until I have seen the entire thing and clarified any questions I may have. I think you will like the concept."

"Roger that; see you next week," Alan said before signing off.

When Miguel got there, Alan called him into his office and closed his door. "Miguel, how are you doing?"

"Great. Is everything OK?"

"I want to ask you who bought the Dodge K-cars I pulled off that old LST."

"I meant to talk to you about that. A local salvage company wanted to buy the cars. The invoice price was sixty-five hundred dollars per car. They offered two thousand dollars. I sent a telex to the Sea Secure claims manager in New York. He approved it, and the sale was completed. I then got a call from the claims guy telling me he had a big problem. Dodge had advised the rental-car company that the cars needed to be destroyed and couldn't be sold. I went back to the salvage company, and they advised they had already sold the cars, and they were no longer in Puerto Rico. I meant to mention this to you, but you were traveling, and I forgot. Is it a problem now?"

"They were sold in the Dominican Republic. They are broken down and abandoned all over the place. There is a very pissed-off army colonel who is looking for the seller."

"Thanks for the heads-up."

"Not your fault, Miguel. You did all the right things. I'll call the head of claims and let him know where they can find the cars. You don't have anything to worry about."

The week was quiet, and Alan flew up to DC the following Monday morning. He was picked up by a car and was delivered to

Langley. Alan went directly to Robert's office, and Eileen brought him directly in.

"How was your trip?" Robert asked.

"Good. No problems."

"We are meeting with the top guy in thirty minutes. He wants to run over this plan and its options directly with you."

"Wow, I'm surprised."

"He has spent a great deal of time on this issue. He considers you one of the top black-ops guys in the entire company and wants to make sure you are safe."

"Can you give me any clues?"

"No. He wants to review this directly with you. I have already given my input. Let's head on up."

They sat quietly in the outer office of the Directorate of Operations. Within ten minutes the executive assistant brought them into the office.

"Alan, great to see you," the director said. "It's been a while. Congratulations on the Distinguished Intelligence Cross for your work in Colombia. Well deserved. How are you doing, not counting a bounty on you by a Venezuelan crime syndicate?"

They all chuckled.

"Great, sir. Very much want to get this resolved."

"Understood. So do we. Have a seat."

"First, we have spent a great deal of time and resources trying to determine the best way to bring this to closure. I had Robert and the teams consider anything that would assure you were safe and could remain an active asset in Puerto Rico. I have been scolded by my executive assistant for spending too much time on this issue. I want to lay out how we got to this point so I can present what I believe is the best course of action. I look forward to your comments and thoughts."

"Thank you, sir, I greatly appreciate the work by you and everyone else."

"First, we start with the fact that there's no limit on cost or assets we will use to make sure this is successfully resolved. We looked at everything from using SEALs again, AC-130 Specter gunships, and air strikes, to name a few. The problem with all of them is they prove you are a valuable US asset for that kind of response, as almost occurred in Colombia. We got away with Colombia, but I don't want to take that chance again. That has the potential of having both the Russians and Cubans after you as well. I looked over all our wet assignments, especially yours, that were designed to look like accidents or bad luck and decided this will be the best course of action. This will assure we keep you under the radar of the Russians and Cubans and prevent endless retaliations by the crime syndicate. I believe the best approach is a hybrid, small operation with unlimited budget and assets. The goal is to assure each of the five wet-work actions on the crime-syndicate heads appears to be an accident or bad luck."

The director paused a minute, waiting for any comment from Alan. Alan nodded his head, waiting for more details.

"So the next questions are who will head up this operation, and who will do the actual wet work? After a great deal of discussion, the consensus was that Robert should lead the operation. He has the most firsthand information on everything that has happened. The real issue and discussion is what agent or agents should we use for the wet work? You are by far our best asset, but you also are the target of the crime syndicate and have a live bounty of three hundred fifty thousand US dollars. Now we want to hear from you."

"Well, sir, I agree one hundred percent," Alan said. "I have the same two goals: safety and remaining a viable asset. If I can get in-depth intel and can work with the backroom boys, we can see what potential exposure I might have in taking out each of the five syndicate leaders. If at all possible, I want to do this myself. If we have any situations where the best opportunity appears to have undue risk for me, I think we look at other options to complete the wet

work. I would like to try to do the wet work outside of Venezuela, but that may not be possible. Whatever you need from me, I am ready."

"I like this approach. We need to do deep intel on each of the five syndicate leaders, just as if it were an independent Absolute Resolution for each, and then decide, as you outlined. I plan to keep your surveillance and backup until this entire issue is resolved and all five syndicate leaders have been eliminated. Since these will all be accidents or bad-luck causes, we don't need to worry about an accelerated time unless circumstances arise. Robert, any thoughts or comments?"

"I'm in full agreement with this approach."

"Great; let's get started now," the director said. "Both of you go meet with the backroom boys and get the background intel requirements set. I am allocating three of my best to be dedicated to this project." The director shook each of their hands.

Over the next four hours, Alan and Robert laid out all the parameters for the intel with the backroom planning team.

The next day Alan and Robert attended the opening ceremony for the Vietnam Veterans Memorial. It was an extraordinary event, with thousands of 'Nam veterans attending. Alan and Robert stayed for the full ceremony that included music, prayer and a color guard. Senator John Warner of Virginia made an excellent keynote speech.

"How about I buy you a beer?" Robert said as they were heading to the Metro.

"Sounds good."

They took the Metro back to the Pentagon station and walked to the Radisson Hotel, where Alan was staying and Robert had parked. They went in the bar, which was empty, and took a table in the back of the room. Robert bought two Heinekens before sitting down with Alan.

"Well, looks like we are all in agreement; I thought you would like the concept."

"I do; I was actually of the same mind before the meeting," Alan replied quietly.

"So was I. That is why he is the top guy. He has really spent a great deal of time on this for you and has opened the floodgates to give us whatever we need to resolve this issue. The three backroom guys assigned to obtain intel and plan are the best in the department. Your continued surveillance and backup are a strong statement of the director's commitment as well."

They finished their beers and shook hands.

"Let's get this done," Alan said.

Alan flew back to San Juan in the morning. He could not shake off his concern on the flight home.

CHAPTER 18

RED OR WHITE?

The next two weeks in Puerto Rico were quiet, both for Sea Secure and the CIA work. Alan was looking at adding another consultant to the Sea Secure staff and also took care of the K-car issue. He called the director of claims for Sea Secure, a friend, and told him the flooded-and-salvaged-car story. The claims director called the Dodge risk manager and let him know about the flooded cars. Dodge sent a small team down to the Dominican Republic, looked up all the last registered owners of the K-cars, and paid each twenty-five hundred dollars. They also arranged for all the abandoned cars to be picked up and delivered to a local scrapyard. The Sea Secure claims director let Alan know the resolution.

Liz also had called to say she had a three-day trip down to Puerto Rico to meet with staff members of the governor to finalize the tax-incentive offers for the new proposed operation. Liz stayed with Alan, and they had a really great time together. On the last night they were at the condo, and Alan was preparing to barbeque steaks after a late afternoon bodysurfing after work and Liz's last meeting.

Alan poured two glasses of champagne to start the evening and came out to the balcony, where Liz was sitting, taking in the breathtaking view of the white beach, palm trees, and aquamarine water that turned dark navy blue a quarter mile off the beach.

"You certainly live in an amazing place. I never get tired of this view."

"Neither do I," Alan said as he handed her the glass of champagne. They touched glasses and took sips.

"Can we talk about your fiancée?"

"I really don't want to. She had a tragic accident, and I was desperately in love with her. Not much else to say."

"I understand," Liz said. "I have never been in love or really deeply cared about a man until I met you. I understand and accept the fact you deeply loved her. I am so sorry you lost her. But I am here now, and I really love you, and I hope you will love me. I'm not trying to put pressure on you; I just want you to know I love you and hope we will continue to see each other. I don't need any commitment from you other than I hope you will keep seeing me. We can work our way through this; I am all in for you."

Alan sat quietly for a minute before he spoke. "Liz, I was hoping we could have a no-strings-attached relationship. Right now that is all I am capable of. I have been worried about our relationship as I did not want to hurt you. I don't want to mislead you. I am not ready now, and I can't see myself changing anytime in the future. It is just where I am right now. I don't want you to believe anything else."

"I understand, Alan. I am so sorry. I don't want you to feel I am pressuring you or that I can't accept a no-strings-attached situation." Liz came over and sat in Alan's lap. "Let's hit the reset button. I really enjoy my time with you, and that is all that matters."

They turned in for the night, both wishing the evening had gone differently.

The next morning Alan took Liz to the airport and walked her to the gate. When they announced first-class boarding, Liz hugged

Alan and gave him a kiss. "I hope we can see each other again soon. Take care of yourself."

""You too, Liz. Have a safe flight back."

On the drive back to his office, Alan pondered how best to move forward with Liz. In his heart he knew Liz was not ready for "no strings attached" and apparently never would be.

Alan's pager went off when he arrived at his office; it was Robert.

"We have some progress on the project. The planning guys identified a top target and what they are calling the low-hanging fruit. Rodrigo Hernandez, one of the crime syndicate's five top guys, has been targeted. He is the finance guy for the syndicate. He also owns an import company that specializes in French wines. Six times a year he travels to Bordeaux, France, to pick his latest wines. Actually, the trip is as much about spending a week with his French girlfriend, who is a flight attendant for Air France. He always stays at the Grand Hotel in Bordeaux for the week and uses the Spa every day before spending the afternoons tasting wine. Rough life."

"What is the timing?"

"He will be there next week. The best 'kill' idea of the week was from one of the planners. He suggested we just tell his wife he has a French girlfriend, and she will kill him," Robert said, laughing.

"That is a good one."

"So the planning guys want you to start growing a mustache and beard today. We will have you fly here before flying to London. We have a company jet scheduled to fly to London on the same day you have to leave, so you can catch a ride over. We are teaming you up with a British company black-ops agent. She is top-notch and has an outstanding reputation at Langley. You will be posing as newlyweds on your honeymoon. The planning guys have reviewed her file and said you owe them for this plan; I'm afraid to ask what that means. Logistics will send you a ticket to get you here in four days. You and your new 'wife' will leave London the day after you arrive. You will fly into Paris and then train down to Bordeaux. I don't want to go into any more detail until you get here."

"Roger that."

"The best part of this first hit is he is the guy who insisted they keep the bounty on you and continue to plan on giving you up to the Russians and Cubans after they torture you. We are sure he still believes you are a US agent and the cause of all their problems. We hope getting rid of him early will reduce the push on your bounty."

"Well, that sounds like good news. See you next week," Alan replied.

The rest of the week was quiet. Alan's beard and mustache, after six days, had grown out quite a bit. Ana joked with him that he needed to shave it. Alan told Ana the big boss wanted him to go to London to sit in on the Sea Secure reinsurance treaty and that he would be gone for a week.

He caught the flight up to Dulles in the morning and was at Langley in the afternoon. Robert sent him to meet with the planning team, who gave Alan an entire brief of all the intel and planning info. He was sent next to the department that handled fake passports and altering visual appearance. They lightened his dark brown hair, beard, and mustache before they took his new passport photo. He was going to be Bill Edwards, an investment banker from New York. His wife's name was Chelsea. The new passport had travel visas and entry and departure stamps from around the world. The photo, with full beard and his hair lightened, made him look very different.

The next morning Alan's car picked him up at 6:30 a.m., and he was at Dulles right on time. The company car had clearance to drop him off at the hangar. They were just pulling the Hawker 700B out of the hangar. Alan saw the captain standing near the hangar door reading the paperwork.

"Captain, I'm catching a ride with you. I'm Alan Joubert. Anyone else on this flight?"

The captain started to laugh. "Do you know who you are hitching a ride with?"

"No. I was just told I was on the flight."

"You're flying over to London with the director of the CIA."

"Wow, had no idea; thanks," Alan replied. He walked over and waited quietly in the hangar door.

A few minutes later, the director's SUV, with an escort SUV, pulled up to the hangar. The director, with another man and woman, got out of the SUV and walked over to the aircraft.

"Ready to go, John?"

"Yes, sir, and your additional passenger, Mr. Joubert, is right over there."

The director waved Alan over, and they all boarded and were airborne in twenty minutes. Alan sat in one of the front seats, while the director and the others were in the rear of the aircraft.

A half hour into the flight, the director called up to Alan, "Legend, come back and visit." Alan moved back, and the director showed him a seat across from him. "Well, good to see you again. Your performance in Colombia was remarkable. If you had not been there, I fear we would have lost all the SEALs. I heard you picked up the ambush before the Colombians warned us."

"I was lucky, sir. I was also with the best of the best."

"Better to be lucky than good. I want you to meet Bob and Linda, two of my assistants."

"Pleasure to meet you."

Both just nodded to Alan.

"I understand you are on your way to take care of one of these crime-syndicate guys. I would say good luck, but you don't need it. Congratulations on your Distinguished Service Cross; well deserved."

For the rest of the flight, the director and staff worked, and Alan went back to his front seat and took a nap. The fight was right on time. The director gave Alan a ride to the US embassy in London.

CHAPTER 19

MEET YOUR NEW WIFE

When he got to the embassy, Alan was led to a conference room to meet with the CIA station manager. There were two women sitting at the conference table, and they both immediately stopped talking when Alan entered the room.

"Have a seat, Alan. I am Station Chief Laura Stanton," the older woman said, smiling. "I have heard a great deal about you. I understand your nickname is The Legend?"

"What can I say?" Alan replied with a big smile.

The other woman was in her early thirties and was absolutely beautiful. Dark, curly hair and extraordinary blue eyes; she was a knockout. She didn't even crack a smile.

"Alan, this is Natalie, your new wife," Laura said with a chuckle.

"Pleasure to meet you, Natalie."

"Same," Natalie said. "Let's run through the intel so I know exactly what you need. I understand this is your mission, and I am along for support."

"That isn't the way I work. I'll make a final decision on how to carry out the mission after we're there and have a chance to get a good feel on the best options. This is all about an iron-clad accident."

"OK. Anything else we need to discuss?"

"Do you like your cover first name?"

"Yes. I checked my passport, and it is perfect. We were just married in East Sussex, and we are on our honeymoon. I am English, and you, of course, are an American. We met at graduate school at Princeton. You were studying finance, and I was studying management. You are now a New York investment banker, and I work for a software company, managing the administrative services. I will act like I am crazy in love with you once we get there. Does that cover everything for the ground rules?"

"That's a great start," Alan replied with a smile. "I can't wait to see you make the transition to crazy in love."

"Don't worry, mate; I will make it happen."

The station chief could hardly keep a straight face during the entire exchange. "Well, I'll leave you two lovebirds together to chat. Let me know if you need anything else before you leave tomorrow. You will be sleeping here—separate rooms, and you will have a car to Heathrow in the morning at zero seven thirty. Your new clothes and suitcases are in your rooms. The cafeteria has eggs, ham, and chips—or French fries, as we call them," Laura finished, unable to contain her smile. She got up and walked out, closing the door behind her.

Alan and Natalie sat quietly for several minutes before Alan finally said, "Let me give you a brief on me. I almost always work alone, and I have pulled off quite a few 'accidents.' I was surprised I was going to have a partner, but I understand I'm lucky to have you. Give me just a brief on you."

"I always work alone," Natalie said. "I was very surprised when I got this assignment. I have heard through the grapevine you are first class, so I am along for the ride. I am a black belt in karate, expert marksman with both pistols and rifles, and have been in black ops for five years—ex-SAS. I will follow your instructions to the letter of the law; just be precise. If I have any questions, you will certainly hear them. I will also have your back one hundred percent and expect exactly the same from you."

"Well, sounds like we are in lockstep. You can bet I'll have your back. We are going to have to make people believe we are in love; are you comfortable with that part?"

"Don't give that part a second thought."

"Excellent; how about I buy you dinner?"

Alan and Natalie went to the cafeteria and had dinner and some light talk with some role playing. She was five foot seven and statuesque, with a very athletic build. They finished up and headed to their rooms, which were side by side. Natalie pulled Alan to her and kissed him with authority. "Sleep well, darling. Looking forward to the honeymoon," she said. Then she walked into her room and closed the door.

Alan walked into his room and sat on the edge of his bed. He could not help chuckling. Well, this was going to be interesting on many different levels. It was clear she could easily take care of herself. She was used to working alone, just as Alan was, so Alan understood why she was not happy. It was absolutely clear she was a professional. Not a bad kisser. Great body.

There was a suitcase rack in the corner of the room with a brand-new, expensive leather suitcase. Alan walked over and quickly went through the packed clothes. All tailor-made slacks, shirts, sports jackets, blazers, and suits, as well as resort casual clothes. There was also a full toilet kit with all high-end products. Hanging on a hook on the wall were tailored gray pants, a white collared shirt with French cuffs, and a blue blazer with gold buttons. On the nearby dresser was a gold Rolex watch, still in the box, two sets of gold cufflinks, and a gold wedding band. *Well, I'll certainly look like a New York investment banker; can't wait to see Natalie.*

CHAPTER 20

GRAND HOTEL BORDEAUX

The next morning Alan got dressed and closed up his suitcase. The pants, shirt, and blazer fit like a glove. The Alan Edmonds European size forty-seven dress loafers fit perfectly. *I am starving.*

Alan headed down the stairs to the first-floor cafeteria and got quite a few curious looks when he walked in. The maître d' escorted Alan to the executive dining room in the back. Natalie was sitting at a table in the corner. As Alan walked over, she stood up and moved to meet him. She looked absolutely beautiful and extremely elegant. She wore a tailored gray-print designer dress that hit above her knees and high heels, and she was loaded with jewelry, including a gold Rolex watch. She immediately gave Alan a hug and a long kiss. "Good morning, darling. I'm so excited about the honeymoon," she said with a sly, flirtatious smile.

They briefly chatted about their travel arrangements during breakfast. Alan noticed the wedding band with diamonds and a very large—probably over two-and-a-half-karat—engagement ring. The planning guys had really gone all out. They both certainly looked the part.

The trip on British Airways to Charles de Gaulle airport was uneventful. They fit in very well in the first-class cabin. The car was waiting to take them to the Paris Montparnasse station for the train to Bordeaux. The car driver was from the CIA station in Paris and gave Alan the small leather duffel with the Berettas, silencers, and ammunition he had ordered for the assignment. The high-speed train to Bordeaux was a first-class car and ran on time. The car from the Grand Hotel was waiting to pick them up.

They were treated like royalty when they were checking in; the suite was magnificent. A bottle of champagne was waiting on ice, with fresh fruit and chocolates. "I could get used to this," Natalie said with a chuckle.

"No kidding. OK, today is only about the lay of the land. I have us booked into the Spa for ninety-minute stone massages so we can take a real close look at the layout."

"I can handle that, darling," she said. She hugged Alan and gave him a deep, long kiss. When she pulled back, she had a wicked smile. "Just got to practice and stay in character," she said. "Let's have some champagne before we get the massage."

"No champagne now; let's change, go to the Spa, and get some steam before the massages."

The steam rooms were separated in the men's and woman's locker rooms. Alan took a twenty-minute steam before showering, putting on the robe, and going to the relaxation room to wait for his massage. Natalie was already in the room reading a magazine. Alan sat down in a chair across from her and picked up a yachting magazine. In ten minutes the attendant came to get them. "Per the request of the lady, you are going to have a signature couple's massage. Follow me."

They were brought into the massage room that had two massage tables. The attendant instructed them to take off their robes and lie on the tables facedown under the sheets. The attendant left, and Natalie immediately took off her robe and hung it on the hook on the door. She had a magnificent body: not an ounce of fat; a C-plus cup size; strong, muscular, shapely legs; and a sculptured core with about a twenty-three-inch waist. She slowly walked to the table and stood holding the sheet. "Are you going to get on the table, darling?" she said with a sly smile.

Alan pulled off his robe and hung it on the door. Then he climbed on his table, facedown, and pulled up the sheet. She lay down, pulled up the sheet, and rested on one elbow. "Very impressive," she said before lying down.

The hot-rock massages were exceptional—ninety minutes of bliss. They showered after and went back to their suite.

"I think I have found the perfect place: the steam room. He always takes steam before and after his massage. The steam room is ten feet by ten feet, all tile, two-tier stacked-bench seating. When the steam recharges, you can barely see in the steam room. No one was in the men's locker room or the steam room. Like all steam rooms, tile floors can be slick. I think this would be a perfect slip-and-fall accident. I could also do it in the shower area, but the steam room would be perfect. Per the intel, we have his normal predicable time for his Spa visit before he leaves for wine tasting in the late afternoon."

"That sounds very promising. His French girlfriend does go with him to the Spa on their first day. He always gives her a bunch of cash to go shopping after that. The next two days, she skips the Spa and goes shopping. I could bump into her and keep her out longer," Natalie replied.

"That makes a lot of sense. He could go hours without being found as long as you had her out and distracted until she had to meet him in the early evening to go wine tasting."

"OK, we are booked for the exact same Spa time tomorrow for one more test run, as well as the next three days. I am going to go for a run before dinner."

"I need a run myself," Alan said. "Wait and I will change and go with you."

They went for a three-mile run outlined by the concierge. Alan was amazed at how athletic Natalie was; she ran stride for stride with him for the first two and half miles and then sprinted the last half mile side by side with Alan. They both caught their breath outside the front door of the Grand. The concierge came out with towels for them.

They went up, showered, and dressed and were ready for the reservation at the gourmet Le Pressoir d'Argent restaurant. Alan wore a white linen dinner jacket, gray collared shirt, and black slacks. Natalie wore a form-fitting black designer dress with a straight skirt well above her knees and high heels. They both caught the eyes of all the men and women as they entered. The maître d' took Natalie by the arm to lead her to their table. The meal and the wine were superb. They went back to the suite after dinner.

Alan stripped down and crawled into the bed in the main bedroom. "You should sleep in this bed; honeymooners don't sleep in separate bedrooms."

"Works for me," she said as she undressed and crawled naked into the bed. "Stay on your side of the bed, mate; remember, I am a black belt," she said with a chuckle.

"Roger that."

The next day was a repeat of the previous day. Alan was all alone in the steam room before his massage. Tomorrow and the next day he hoped it would just be him and Rodrigo Hernandez.

The next day went exactly as planned. Alan ended up in the steam room with Hernandez, and Liz was with his French girlfriend. Hernandez and his girlfriend looked exactly like the intel photos. Alan gave a brief hello when he entered the steam room and climbed to the top bench, sitting to the right above Hernandez. Alan left after fifteen minutes, and Hernandez spent his typical twenty minutes in the steam after his massage. Natalie and Hernandez's French girlfriend were chatting and laughing in the relaxation waiting room. The Spa staff then came and got Alan and Natalie, and Natalie and the girlfriend said their good-byes, with kisses on each cheek. This time Alan and Natalie both immediately hung the robes and climbed on the tables for more first-class hot-stone massages. Then they dressed and went back to their suite.

"I have her all set for shopping, lunch, and more shopping tomorrow. I asked her if she had a shopping budget, and she said no. I told her I didn't either. I expect I can keep her out until she has to get back to change for the wine tasting."

"Great. I climbed up on the top bench in the steam room, and he never even flinched. I'll be in the perfect position to take him down. The backroom guys checked the Spa schedule, and it is only the two of us tomorrow. Tomorrow is the day."

"You bet, mate; let's do it."

The next morning Alan left for the Spa, and Natalie went to meet the girlfriend in the lobby. Natalie looked absolutely magnificent in a red designer dress above her knees and wedge high-heeled shoes. She had on all of the jewelry and the Rolex and carried a Louis Vuitton bag; she certainly looked the part. In the elevator Natalie pulled Alan to her and gave him a deep kiss. "See you later, darling. I'll try not to spend all your money." Another couple was in the elevator, and they both smiled.

Alan got out of the elevator at the Spa floor, and Natalie gave him a sexy, flirtatious smile and blew him a kiss. "Good-bye, my love."

Alan walked into the Spa, and no one was at the front desk. He checked the appointment book, and Hernandez was getting his massage and would be out in thirty minutes. Alan went into the men's locker room and picked one of the lockers set up for incoming guests. He undressed and tied a towel tightly around his waist using a square knot. Then he pulled on the robe and slipped on the flip-flops. He sat in a toilet stall, waiting for Hernandez to come back from the massage. Alan heard the door open and waited several seconds before opening the door a crack to confirm it was Hernandez. It was an employee, putting in more towels and checking to make sure everything was in good order. At that moment, Hernandez came into the locker room.

"Do you need anything, sir? How was your massage?"

"Excellent; I should marry her," he said, and they both started to laugh.

"You are very funny, sir. If you need anything, just alert the Spa front desk using the telephone on the wall," the attendant replied before leaving.

Hernandez hung his robe and entered the steam room. Alan waited two minutes and then walked over and hung his bathrobe on the hook outside the steam room before going inside. Hernandez looked up when Alan entered and nodded, and Alan nodded back and again climbed to the second bench and waited. Alan was three feet away from Hernandez and three feet higher. After five minutes, when the steam had just recharged, Alan stood up, took one step over, and quickly grabbed Hernandez in a chokehold. Hernandez was only about five foot nine inches and probably one hundred and sixty pounds; there was minimal struggling before he lost consciousness. Then Alan violently twisted his head, breaking his neck. He lifted Hernandez to the floor of the steam room and laid him down with his head toward the first tile bench. Alan lifted Hernandez's head and forcefully struck his forehead against the corner of the tile bench.

Alan left the steam room, wiping down the door handles with his towel. The locker room was still empty. He moved quickly to the relaxation waiting room for his massage. The attendant came for him within minutes for his massage. After the ninety-minute massage, Alan went back to the locker room. It was still empty, and there was no sign Hernandez had been discovered. Alan changed and signed the bill at the front desk on the way out. He went to the lobby bar and ordered a beer. He sat and sipped it for a half hour, chatting with the bartender, before going up to the room.

At 4:30 p.m. the room telephone rang. "Hello," Alan said.

"Bill, I'm still out shopping and will be another hour. Is that OK?"

"Sure. Everything is fine here; see you later in the room. Enjoy. Hope you don't spend too much," he said with a chuckle. "See you soon."

An hour and a half later, Alan heard the three hard knocks, three light knocks, and one hard knock; Alan had taught her that code. Alan moved to the side of the door as the key turned and the door opened. Natalie came in with six shopping bags, three in each hand. "Do you think they will let me keep all of this? Everything fits me perfectly," she said with a smile.

Alan described the events of the afternoon. "How did it go with you?"

"Well, I have a new best friend. She poured her soul out to me. She knows Hernandez does something illegal and knows he is married with a wife and two kids. She has been seeing him for three years, ever since he flew on one of her flights and talked her into going to dinner. He pays for her high-end apartment and sends her five thousand US dollars a month as well. These trips, of course, are regular events and always include wild shopping sprees; she had twice as many bags as I did and spent a small fortune—all cash. She wanted me to go with her tomorrow. I told her you and I had planned wine tours, and I wanted to be alone with you. She laughed and said she didn't blame me. She wanted to know if you were as good in bed as you looked. Quite a day. Any fight back, problems, or loose ends?"

"No. It went down just as planned. He didn't have a chance; it was over in a couple of minutes. No problems, no loose ends."

"Well, now we get three more days; we can't leave, as it would be suspicious."

Alan and Natalie went to dinner that night and still had not heard anything about the "accident." There was no sign of the girlfriend. They had champagne to start, with oysters, excellent Dover sole, and a bottle of Chardonnay. After dinner they went for a nightcap at the lobby bar. They sat at the bar, and the same bartender from earlier waited on them. "Hello again. What can I get you?" she asked.

"We will both have cognacs. Thank you," Alan ordered.

The bartender set the drinks down and said to Alan, "Have you heard about the gentleman who fell and died in the Spa steam room?"

"No. When did that happen?"

"Sometime today—they're not sure when. They didn't find him until the woman traveling with him reported he was missing. They found him in the steam room; he had fallen, hit his head, and broken his neck. Police determined it was an accident. The hotel is keeping it very quiet; they don't want bad publicity. Don't tell anyone I told you."

"Wow," Alan said. "Don't worry. That's shocking. I certainly will make sure I'm careful in the steam room."

"Let's take these back to the room, darling," Natalie said with a sexy smile. She picked up her glass of cognac and stood up.

Alan opened the door, and Natalie was right behind him. He put down his cognac next to the bed. She put down her cognac next to his and wrapped her arms around his neck. Then she pushed him on the bed, fell on top of him, and kissed him deeply. The tension had been building from when they first met. An hour and a half later, they both lay breathless. "Well, I guess we broke the rules," she said with a very sated smile.

"What do you mean 'we'? I was ensnared," Alan said not able to stop laughing. She gave him a big swat on the leg and wrapped herself around him. They were asleep in a very short time.

The rest of the trip was outstanding; it was a tough job having to live the life of the rich and famous. The CIA car picked them up as scheduled to take them to Charles de Gaulle for the flight back. Alan returned the small duffel with the Berettas and advised they were still clean. Natalie fell asleep on his shoulder on the flight. Their car was waiting to take them to the US embassy when they landed in London. They turned in the watches and all the jewelry. Both were surprised to be told they should keep the clothes and suitcases. They ate dinner and went to their rooms to turn in. Outside their rooms, Natalie wrapped her arms around Alan's neck and kissed him deeply. "Well, mate, it has been a real pleasure. If you get back to London, call me."

"You can bet on it, mate; take care of yourself," Alan replied with a chuckle before closing his door.

Alan shaved after he showered in the morning. He had an early flight out of Heathrow on British Airways, business class. He slept the entire flight back after one Bloody Mary and the company-issued little blue international travel pill. He connected through Dulles and was back at his condo at 7:30 p.m. on Sunday. His pager went off four times, all Ana. *I'm going bodysurfing. I'll deal with all this tomorrow.*

CHAPTER 21

ONE DOWN, FOUR TO GO

Alan was in the office early as usual, and he closed his door and called Robert.

"Robert here."

"Well, that was really some interesting planning, but it worked perfectly. Tell the backroom team that was a Picasso. No loose ends, no issues, and everything went exactly as planned."

"We have a copy of the police investigation, and they did do a cursory autopsy; it was declared an accidental slip and fall. The body was accidentally cremated before it was shipped back; we had that done. I heard from the London station chief that you and your partner were grand entertainment. Did she come through when it counted?"

"She sure did. I would work with her any time in the future. Did you see her file?"

"Yes. That is why we picked her. I also saw her photos; now I understand why the planning guys said you owed them. Seven days in a high-end resort on a honeymoon with that babe? And we paid you?" he said with a chuckle.

"They had me keep the high-end tailored clothes as well."

"The backroom planning team had a pool on whether you would get lucky. I understand the cameras they planted in your suite allowed a winner to be declared before they were erased—or at least allegedly erased. Don't worry. We asked you to act like newlyweds; I understand you both get an A plus on that task."

"Damn. I looked and didn't see them. Where were the cameras? You tell the backroom gang they'd better be erased. They don't want to get on my bad side."

"The cameras were in the crystal chandeliers in each room. You would have never found them; new tools from the tech guys. Apparently erasing for their future safety was the unanimous consensus; I do believe they are erased. Take it easy on them. You'll be happy to know we have the number-two target. This was the other guy who was all-in to get you; he is in our crosshairs. The backroom team is putting together a plan as we speak. I'll give you a heads-up as soon as we have a schedule."

"Wow. It would be great to get the second-most aggressive guy after me. Let me know," Alan said before signing off.

Ana saw he was off the phone and knocked on the door shortly after he hung up. "Hey, boss. How was London?"

"It was great. I bought you a gift. You have been doing an outstanding job holding down the fort while I've been gone," he said as he handed her the box, which contained a beautiful dark-gray pearl necklace.

"Boss, you didn't have to do this, but I greatly appreciate the thoughtfulness. Thank you so much."

"You deserve it. So what is with all the pages?"

"Three of them were for Liz. She had a last-minute trip to Puerto Rico. After the third message, I called her back and let her know you were in London and out of contact and would not be back until the weekend. She was only here three days and arrived the day after you left."

"OK. What else?"

"The one fire we had was taken care of by Miguel. You have a pile of files and messages on your desk; nothing is urgent. You have an interview this afternoon with the new guy applying for the consultant job. Thank you so much for the pearl necklace," she said as she closed his door on the way out.

Alan called Liz as soon as Ana left.

"Hey, Liz. I'm back in Puerto Rico."

"Oh wow. I had a last-minute trip to Puerto Rico and was very disappointed you were in London. Your assistant is a jewel. She let me know you were tied up."

"The big guy sent me to London to see how they put together our reinsurance. It was a very productive trip."

"I'll be coming back next Monday. Will you be around? The new manufacturing location is looking really good."

"Right now it looks like I'll be here. Given what I do, you never know."

"I know. OK, if you are there, can I stay with you? Does that work for you?"

"Of course; I'll confirm on Sunday night. You're always welcome."

"Excellent. I'll have my fingers crossed. Take care, sweetheart," she said and signed off.

The next several days were quiet. The following day Alan called Robert.

"Anything cooking for the next week?"

"No, but probably soon after. The planning guys are almost finished, and the target window looks like about two weeks."

"Roger that; I have a guest coming down Monday for a few days. Thanks for the continued surveillance and backup. I can almost relax," he said.

Monday Alan left work an hour early to pick Liz up at the airport. She looked beautiful, as usual. She had her long blonde hair in a ponytail and was wearing black slacks and a white silk blouse. They drove directly to Alan's condo, and Liz kissed him and dragged him back immediately to the bedroom. They both lay breathless after a very athletic hour. "Wow, did I miss you," she said quietly. "I guess you were too busy to miss me."

"I *was* busy," he replied in a careful measured tone, again feeling uneasy.

They went bodysurfing for an hour. Alan picked up both his surveillance and backup at the beach. The woman handling surveillance was sitting on a bench at the entrance to the beach with a dog on a leash. The backup man was in a beach chair approximately one hundred feet away. After surfing, Alan barbequed steaks on the Weber with a bottle of Saint-Émilion Bordeaux he had bought on his trip.

The rest of the visit went well. The next night they went to dinner at El Convento and then salsa dancing at La Concha. Liza had been practicing salsa; she was amazing. The next morning Liz was flying out at 11:00 a.m. so Alan stayed home to give her a ride to the airport. Alan had fixed breakfast, and Liz had just finished packing and came out to sit on the balcony. Alan followed her out; the view was extraordinary. The white-sand beach and palm trees looked like a postcard picture.

"So good to see you again, Alan. I want you to know 'no strings' will work for me. I just want to make sure we keep seeing each other."

"Liz, you are world class. I enjoy every minute I spend with you. You will always be welcome here."

"I just don't want that to turn you off. I can't help it. I hope you understand."

"I do, sweetheart; don't worry. I know one thing for sure: I need more time. I can't make any promises. I hope you can live with that. I don't want to hurt you."

"No, I'm fine." Liz said before wrapping her arms around his neck and giving him a kiss.

Alan brought her to the departure gate at the airport, and she again had a tear in her eye as she turned to board.

Alan headed to the office. *This has really gotten complicated. I really enjoy being with Liz, but I'm nowhere near ready to fall in love with her. I don't want Liz putting her life on standby waiting for me. Maybe ending now would be best for Liz.*

Alan's pager went off as soon as he parked; it was Robert. Alan called as soon as he got to his office.

"You paged me?"

"Yes. We have an action time now for the second target. Jorge Diaz owns a company in Venezuela that sells and exports heavy equipment throughout the Caribbean. He has a trip planned in a week and a half; he will be visiting both Haiti and the Dominican Republic. He will be traveling to several small towns in the mountains, besides Port-au-Prince and Santo Domingo, visiting distributors and large customers. He has girlfriends in both Haiti and DR. The planning group is working hard on getting the cleanest and safest options for you to make a final decision in the field. We are going to set you up in Haiti with your old Phoenix buddy, Rene, to cover your back. We're still deciding on the Dominican Republic; we may consider also using Rene."

"That would work for me. Rene also speaks Spanish fluently, besides French."

"I saw that in his file; I'll let you know. The top guy wants you to have someone to cover your back. We believe the first operation was clean, but we are not taking any chances. This guy travels with an assistant who may also be part of the crime syndicate."

"Roger that; I'll make sure that time is open," he said and then signed off.

Alan had dinner the next night with Marta and Federico. It was great seeing them both. They only mentioned Maria when he was leaving, letting him know they continued to get better and only remembered the good times. Alan was still struggling with his grief but did not want to let them know. He hoped his emotions didn't show when Maria's dad gave him a sudden hug good-night. "Take care, Federico," Alan said in a husky voice and then walked away quickly.

Meme/

CHAPTER 22

HAITI OR DOMINICAN REPUBLIC?

The next day Alan's pager went off on his drive into the office. He called Robert as soon as he got in. "What's up?"

"We now have firm dates for Diaz. He will first be in Haiti next Monday. He will be there for four days, and then he will be flying out of Port-au-Prince to Santo Domingo. He will be staying in the DR for four days as well. Planning guys have his full itinerary, every detail. Just wanted to give you a definitive timeline; backroom guys are feverishly working on multiple options. I have decided your backup will be Rene in both Haiti and the DR. He's the obvious choice, considering your work on Phoenix together and your off-the-grid work last year. Does that work for you?"

"Totally; would only trade him for Natalie," Alan said with a laugh.

"I bet you would. I'll have to let Rene know he was your second choice," he said with a snicker. "We will have a reason for you to be in both places for Sea Secure. Rene will be a tourist in the DR if it is not over in Haiti."

"Roger that; I'm ready to move a step closer to conclusion. Is there a chance the other three might just forget about me?"

"It's a possibility. We would need this next one to end up with another iron-clad accident, and I expect it is possible."

"OK. It will be great to be working with Rene again," Alan said before they signed off.

The next several days were quiet.

When he got back to the condo after work on the third day, there were two messages on the answering machine. The first was from Liz asking Alan to call when he had time. The second call was a hang up.

Alan called Liz at her home, and she picked up after several rings. "Liz."

"How are you?"

"Great. Just wanted to see how you are doing, and frankly, I just miss you."

"All is good."

"I also wanted to talk to you about something strange. I have seen a strange man now three times at different locations. I saw him once outside my house two days ago, yesterday near my office when I went to lunch, and also outside my gym. It just feels creepy. I have never had anything like this happen before."

"Any reason anyone would be doing this—boyfriends, ex-boyfriends, issues at work, or anything like that?"

"No—just appears to be happening out of the clear blue sky. Should I call the police?"

"The problem is that if he has not been threatening or done anything aggressive, they can't do anything. I have a friend in the San Francisco Police Department. I'll call him and ask him to check this out off duty for me. Give me the best description you can and a brief overview of your schedule for the next two days."

Liz had a great eye for detail and had a really good description of the man. When they finished, they said good-byes.

Alan immediately called Robert. "Robert here."

"We may have a problem with the woman I've been dating, Liz, who lives in the San Francisco Bay Area. She believes she is being stalked. She has no logical explanation of why this might be happening. She has visited me several times and stayed at my condo recently. I know it's related to my problem, and we have to make unequivocally sure she is safe. I have a great description of the guy and an overview of her schedule for the next two days. She's seen him three times in the last two days."

"I agree. I don't believe in coincidences. They may have picked up your surveillance and backup and decided to go after a softer target to get to you. I'll get an FBI team outside her house tonight and will shadow her for the next two days. I'll keep you up to speed on anything that comes up. I'll also see if surveillance and backup have picked up anything that has been out of the usual."

Alan provided all the information to Robert. "Thanks, Robert. Really appreciate your support."

The next morning Alan's pager went off at 6:30 a.m. He called Robert back. "What's up?"

"Our team picked up this guy, and he is definitely surveilling Liz. They got a good photo and IDed him, and you're not going to like this. Guy is a known enforcer for the Venezuelan crime syndicate. Your surveillance and backup picked him up in Puerto Rico when Liz was visiting and thought he could be one of their guys. They photoed him, but he never came back, and they didn't see him again, so they wrote him off as a false positive and didn't send in the photo."

"Damn; I can't believe I have put Liz at risk. How good is this guy?"

"This guy is very good. He was a captain in the Venezuelan Special Forces when he got recruited by the syndicate. Extremely well trained and graduated from our officer candidate school."

"Have our guys tracked him back to where he is staying?"

"Yes. He is staying at the Hyatt in Cupertino. He is alone. We got a tracker on his car last night, a rental, so we know exactly when and where he moves. Our top priority, of course, is to make sure Liz is safe. We are trying to figure a way to have this guy disappear without causing even more alarm bells on the crime-syndicate end."

"We need to do that soon; we can't take a chance he gets his hands on Liz."

"Agreed. The problem we have is he is unlike the others they have sent. He is not wanted for anything here or in Venezuela. Law enforcement has no reason to detain him. The good news is everything points to him trying to grab Liz to get to you, not harm her. Our guys saw a pistol when he got out of his car, before he zipped his windbreaker. He doesn't have a permit. I think our best bet now is to stop him for suspicious behavior and find his gun. We can then turn him over to immigration and customs to arrange a quick deportation. Your thoughts?"

"Someone like this is not going away. I'm all right with this as a temporary fix, but once he is outside the US, we have to eliminate him."

"Agreed. Get back to you this afternoon."

Alan's pager went off at 3:15 p.m. He called back right away.

"OK, Alan, the backroom team has a plan," Robert said. "We are using one of our contacts at the FBI to coordinate his arrest, working with his contacts at the SFPD. They should have him this afternoon. Now we need to figure out what we are going to do moving forward with regard to Liz."

"We can always remove my backup and let them take their best shot directly at me. I also have to break up with Liz immediately and hope that helps."

"Top guy won't agree to remove your backup. I agree on the breakup. So sorry, but it will no doubt help to take her off their radar."

"OK. Let me know when it is done. We will need to keep surveillance and backup on her for at least two weeks after this guy is gone. I'll then break up without it looking like it's tied to this issue."

"Agreed. Let me know when you let her know it is over. Thank God she picked this guy up before he could grab her."

"Roger that. Are we still a go on Diaz?"

"Yes. I'll call as soon as this is resolved."

Alan sat quietly after the call. *I will miss Liz, but I can't have her be at risk.*

Alan's pager went off the next day at 11:30 a.m. "Hope you have good news," he said when he called Robert back.

"It's done. He had a Berretta—same model you use—and a silencer. He's being turned over to US Customs Service for deportation tomorrow. They stopped him for suspicious behavior for sitting in his car for two hours waiting for Liz. He was a block from a Wells Fargo bank, and the cops grabbed him and said they had passed him twice in two hours and were suspicious he was preparing to rob the bank. It worked perfectly."

"OK, we have some time now," Alan said. "I want to get rid of Diaz and see what they do next; if I have to take down the last three, as well as this guy, so be it."

Alan called Liz after he hung up. "Liz, my friend on the SFPD ran all the info. He doesn't think you will see him again, but if you do, call me right away."

"Thank you so much, Alan. I have not seen him today, so I hope he's right."

"Glad I could help. I have to run, babe, but call me if you see him," he replied.

On Monday morning Alan caught the Prinair flight to Port-au-Prince. Rene was waiting for him outside immigration and customs. You could not miss him, at 6'2" and 225 pounds. He was a Cajun from Southern Louisiana and was part black, part French and part Cherokee. His close cropped hair was a military cut. They gave each other a hug. "Well, here we go again, my friend," Alan said as they walked to the rental car. They would not be using a car from the embassy. Rene, who had taken a cab to the airport, drove them to the Holiday Inn for Alan to check in.

Rene pulled out his copy of the intel, and they sat at the small table in the corner of Alan's hotel room.

"Have you picked a spot?" Alan led off.

"You bet. Let's see how we match up. I picked the road accident in the mountains near Fond-des-Blancs."

"Damn. Exactly. Did you get the operations shipment?" Alan said with a smile. They did their fist bump, pulled their open hands back like an explosion, and then saluted.

"Got it. The planning guys sent us everything we need for each option in Haiti. You want some even better news? Tomorrow night is going to be a torrential rainstorm in the mountain—made-to-order weather conditions."

"We had a heavy-hitter crime-syndicate guy, former captain Venezuelan Special Forces, apparently try to grab my girlfriend in San Francisco. She spotted him, and Robert had the guy picked up for carrying a firearm without a permit. He had a silencer as well. They turned him over to immigration and customs, and they deported him. I'm hoping after we take down Diaz they will lose interest in me. But it has to be an unquestionable accident—no flaws or loose ends."

"I'll follow Diaz and his assistant from the airport this afternoon and make sure they stick to their itinerary today, tonight, and tomorrow. If they do, we will plan on the operation at twenty-three hundred hours in the mountains. It takes four hours to get to the intercept location; I already scouted the area last week. I'll also trade the car tomorrow for a black four-wheel-drive Jeep."

"Roger that," Alan said as Rene packed up to leave.

"Don't worry; we will get this done," Rene said before heading out.

Alan remained at the hotel that night and was waiting for Rene the next day. He arrived right on time.

"Only good news. He was like Swiss clockwork. The weather is still scheduled for a torrential rainstorm in the mountains. FYI, the assistant is definitely more than just a business associate. The guy has shooter written all over him. Got the Jeep, and all the gear is already loaded. Let's go to my favorite restaurant; then we can hit the road."

They had a great meal at Rene's favorite seafood restaurant before starting the drive to Fond-des-Blancs on schedule. Diaz was heading to a meeting with the United Nations director of construction operations for Haiti. The United Nations was building roads in the area using equipment that was both purchased and leased from Diaz. He was meeting to make sure his leased equipment was going to be used on the next very large road project scheduled for the end of the year.

Alan and Rene arrived at the intercept location two hours before the expected arrival of Diaz. They found the location where they had planned to wait, which gave them full cover from anyone passing on the road. It was just starting to rain. They got out their bright-yellow Haiti Federal Police rain jackets with reflector tape, placed the Haiti Federal Police insignia magnets on both doors, and placed the blue flashing light on the dashboard. They both had their pistols in shoulder holsters, along with their silencers. Finally they pulled out their Federal Police hats with rain covers and were ready to wait in the Jeep until it was time to intercept.

Diaz and his assistant were driving a white Peugeot, and at this time of night, they would definitely be the only vehicle on the road. Alan and Rene waited an hour before they saw headlights coming up the road a mile away. The roads followed old mule trails and circled up and down the mountains. The rain was beginning to come down in a steady downpour. Alan had his infrared scope and clearly picked up a clean sighting of the white Peugeot with a driver and a passenger. "We have a positive sighting. Let's go," he said, pulling his Berretta out and racking a round in the chamber. Rene did the same, and they drove out to the road and parked, blocking both lanes. They turned on the flashing blue light.

They watched as the Peugeot continued to approach and then slowed down when it was about a hundred feet away. The Peugeot slowly pulled up to twenty feet from the Jeep and stopped. Alan had his rain jacket hood pulled up over his hat so his face could not be seen. Rene walked over to the driver's door with a twelve-inch flashlight. The driver rolled down the window right away.

"Gentlemen, we are looking for two men who have abducted a young girl," he began in French. Both men looked at him with confusion, so he switched to English. "Do you speak English?"

"Yes, we do, Officer. Is there a problem?"

"We are looking for two men who have abducted a young girl in Port-au-Prince. We need to ask you to step out of the car; we need to search the car and the trunk."

"Sure, Officer. No problem. I can assure you we are just businessmen going to a meeting with thc United Nations near Fond-des-Blancs," Diaz said. Both men slipped on their rain jackets and got out of the car.

"Thank you, gentlemen. Please wait over by my partner; please give me your keys first," Rene replied. "I need you to walk to our vehicle and place your hands on the hood so my partner can do a quick pat-down."

Both men began walking toward the front of the Jeep. Alan was carefully watching, ready to drop to one knee and pull his Berretta. The men walked up and placed their hands on the Jeep hood. Alan came up behind them and patted down the assistant first and then Diaz; both were clean. Rene had just finished searching the car and came walking over to the Jeep. Both Rene and

Alan were ready to pull their pistols. Alan lined up behind Diaz, and Rene came behind Diaz's assistant.

"I think these are the guys; there was some blood in the trunk," Rene said in French, as planned.

"Is there a problem, Officer?" Diaz asked Rene.

"Yes sir; we do have a problem. How did you get bloodstains in your car trunk?"

"What? Officer, this is a rental car we received at the airport. I can assure you we know nothing about any bloodstains."

"Sir, if this is true, you will not have a problem. We will have to bring you in to our station several miles from here until we straighten all this out. Please place your hands behind your back," Rene commanded as both he and Alan pulled out their handcuffs.

Both men complied, and the handcuffs were attached. "Come back to your car, and my partner will drive your car, so when we have this resolved, you will be ready to leave," Rene said. They walked the men back to their car and put them both in the backseat.

Both Alan and Rene pulled small drug plungers out of their pockets and jammed them into the men's arms. The confused men began to fight to get out of the car and began screaming at them. "What is going on? Why did you do that? Let us go immediately! We are businessmen."

Alan and Rene easily held the handcuffed men down in the backseat of their car. Within minutes the men had stopped struggling.

"OK, let's let the drug fully kick in," Rene said, as now the rain was coming down in buckets. In five minutes they moved both men to the front seat of their car. They removed the handcuffs from both and put on their seatbelts.

"The push-off spot is thirty feet up on the right. It is perfect," he said.

Rene put the car in neutral and released the emergency brake, and they began pushing the car, with the doors open, to the spot

Rene had pointed to on the right. When the car was fifteen feet from the edge of the cliff, Rene pulled the emergency brake to stop the car. Alan walked over to the edge of the cliff; it was a vertical drop down five hundred feet into a rocky gorge. "Perfect; it's even better than the photos."

"On your command, sir," Rene said to Alan. Rene walked over and released the emergency brake, and both men closed the doors.

They both walked to the trunk, and Alan barked, "Now." They began pushing the car as fast as they could toward the cliff's edge. In the fifteen feet to the edge, they got the car moving at about five miles an hour. The car ran off the edge of the cliff, and they watched it plunge five hundred feet to the bottom of the gorge. The rocky ground on the cliff top left no footprints.

"I don't expect the seatbelts helped," Alan said with a chuckle.

Rene could not help laughing. "The UN should build a guard-rail here."

They removed their gloves, stored all their equipment, and drove back to Port-au-Prince; the rain continued to pour. The trip back was long but uneventful, with some flooded road areas.

Rene brought Alan back to the hotel and parked. They went to a local bar down the street.

"I'll buy you a couple of shots of Five-Star Barbancourt," Alan offered. They drank the two shots, and then Rene walked Alan back to the hotel. Alan gave Rene a hug, and then they bumped fists, pulled their hands back like an explosion, and saluted.

"Hope I see you soon, Alan; take care," Rene said.

"Take care of yourself as well. Until next time," Alan replied before heading for his room.

His trip back to Puerto Rico was uneventful.

CHAPTER 23

BREAKING UP IS HARD TO DO

Alan called Robert when he got back to his condo.
"Robert here."

"Well, that was a work of art," Alan said. "It was totally clean—no problem, and no loose ends from our side. They didn't know what was happening. Tell the backroom boys fine job, and let them know I bought each of them a bottle of Five-Star Barbancourt. Any chatter from Venezuela?"

"Not yet, but it is still early. As of this moment, there has been no report of the accident in Haiti. We will be carefully monitoring both in Haiti and in Venezuela. I'll let you know as soon as we get anything in. It sounds like you and Rene made a great team—no big surprise."

"Yeah, it was a typical well-oiled machine. We hardly have to even talk now," Alan said with a chuckle.

The next morning Alan's pager went off at 6:30 a.m.

"We got feedback from Haiti as well as Venezuela. The UN guy called Diaz's office to find out why he did not show up. This triggered their call to the Haitian Police in Port-au-Prince. Their hotel rooms were empty, but all their clothes and travel items were still there. Given their last known destination was Fond-des-Blancs, the matter was turned over to the federal police. There have been several similar accidents at the cliff they went off, which was one of the reasons the backroom boys picked this as one of your options. The federal police found the car and reported back to Diaz's office confirming there was a single-car fatal accident caused by missing a turn and driving off a cliff. They have already closed their file and confirmed the bodies are ready to be shipped back to Venezuela. The feedback from the phone taps on the top crime-syndicate guys looks good. They are just shocked; they can't believe they have lost another guy. There is no indication of any suspicion."

"Well, it all sounds encouraging."

"With these two guys gone, let's hope so. We'll sit back now and see if there are any signs you are still on the radar. The top guys want to keep your surveillance and backup. We will have to pull the surveillance and backup for Liz after the two weeks. I still believe breaking up is the safest course of action until we can confirm you are in the clear further down the road."

"Agreed. I'll do it early next week. I'll let you know. Keep her surveillance and backup a week after I let her know. I'll call you when it is done."

"OK. I'll do that for you, Alan," Robert said and then signed off.

The rest of the week was quiet. Alan only had a day trip to Saint Croix for Sea Secure. Alan had been running through his mind how he would break it to Liz. He enjoyed being with her, but he was not in love with her. This was really going to be difficult. He had not talked to her in a week.

The next day Alan waited until he knew Liz would be home to call her. He had finally decided how he would end it.

"Liz," she answered.

"Hi, Liz. Hope all is well. Still no sign of the guy?"

"Hi, Alan. I'm so glad to hear from you. No sign of the guy. Did your police buddy ever give an explanation of why the man appeared to be stalking me?"

"Nothing for certain, but I'm glad you are aware and alert. Keep that up, but I don't expect you will see that guy again."

"I'm glad you called; I was just getting ready to call you. I'll be in Puerto Rico on Thursday and have two days of work and then plan to stay over the weekend. Will you be around?"

"Liz, we need to talk. I have been really soul-searching, and I believe it may be best for us to take some time off. I am nowhere near ready for a serious relationship, and I don't want to mislead you. You are an amazing woman who deserves to be with someone who can commit to you. I'm not able to now, and I don't know if I'll ever be."

Liz sat quietly for a minute before she responded. "I'm so sorry you feel I have been putting pressure on you."

"It is not your fault at all. I'm just not whole yet, and I can't give you the love you want now or maybe ever. You deserve much, much better. Let's take time off and let me try to resolve my issues. This is my problem, and I have got to resolve it. Let's take six months off. I hope after more time I can heal. I can't make any promises."

"Alan, I do love you. I can't help that; it just happened. I do very much respect your feelings and needs. I hope you understand I just want to spend time with you. I don't care if you ever love me. I hope you understand; I need you to tell me you do understand."

"I do, Liz. I do."

"I want you to know I'll be there for you at any time."

"If you ever need my help, call me."

"OK. Take care of yourself, and I hope you decide we can see each other again without the baggage," Liz said before she said good-bye and hung up.

Alan called Robert next. "Liz and I are done. I just hung up with her."

"How did she take it?"

"She was simply amazing. I know this hurt her deeply, and it really was hard for me as well. I guess the question is, can I have a serious relationship with a civilian while I'm with the Absolute Resolution program?"

Robert sat quietly for a minute, something he seldom did. "I think you decided this question today."

"OK, enough said. Now, where are we on these last three syndicate guys? Do we have any new intel from Venezuela? I want to finalize this one way or another. I still believe we need to take out the guy who tried to grab Liz, both for her safety and mine. Do I still have a three-hundred-fifty-thousand live bounty?"

"Well, the news is not so good. The bounty is still in place. Apparently after the attempted Colombian ambush, the Russians and the Cubans have started to use another crime syndicate to smuggle the weapons. We're tracking the weapons from the origin, and the top guys are about ready to start intercepting right after the cargo moves to Europe for shipment to Venezuela. The crime syndicate has decided again to capture you and try to get the business back. They don't have you linked to their lost partners, thank heavens."

"Well, then let's go get the rest of them."

"Agreed. It's been authorized. The top guy's one proviso is the next action takes out all three of the last syndicate bosses at once. He believes if they 'accidentally' lose one more of their partners, they will no longer believe any were accidents."

"Well, that makes it much more complicated, but I have to agree."

"So stay tuned. The backroom guys have intel that in the near future they will all be meeting to add more partners. We may have the perfect opportunity to get them all at one time."

"OK. I need to remove this sword hanging over my head. Call me as soon as we have something concrete," Alan said.

CHAPTER 24

LET'S GO YACHTING

The next three weeks were quiet. Alan did not have any traveling off the island, and he was now taking the surveillance and backup as business as usual.

Alan had just arrived early at his office when his pager went off.

"You are really going to like this," Robert began. "The backroom guys have pulled off another world-class plan to get not only the last three top crime bosses but also the guy who came after Liz all at one time."

"Tell me more."

"The top guys of the syndicate plan to have a meeting to decide on new partners, and the guy who went after Liz is one of the candidates. They will be meeting with him and two other guys to decide. They are going to be doing it very high-end, chartering a yacht out of Turks and Caicos Islands. They chartered a Palmer Johnson one-hundred-twenty-eight-footer; they got it for an excellent price—from us."

"Oh, this is too good to be true. Please tell me they are not going to bring their own crew."

"They tried to, but we would not charter the yacht bareboat without a crew. They asked for a brief bio of each crew member to review. The backroom guys are building aliases for you, Rene, and Natalie, and we have agents to be an engineer, a chef, two deckhands, and two hostesses. I want to check and see if you wanted to contract with your buddy Fast Eddie to serve as first mate. I know you said he was now working on a large yacht. Your thoughts?"

"Well, this is simply amazing. I can't believe I'll be with Rene and Natalie. I'll bet the ranch we can get Eddie, especially if I ask. He is an excellent choice. What is the timeline?"

"We have a week and a half for you guys to get on board and set up the yacht. All the personnel I'm providing were personally picked by me and are very capable—except for the chief, who serves in our executive dining room here in Langley. The crime-syndicate guys arrive in two and half weeks, so you will have a week. Will that be enough?"

"Yes, I think so. I should call Eddie and go see him right away to get him on board."

"Roger that; call him right away and set up a visit with him. Backroom boys want you to start growing a full beard right away," Robert said before signing off.

Holy smoke. This is just excellent. I'm ready to end this threat. What a team. I know Fast Eddie will jump on board. Looking forward to seeing Natalie again.

Alan called Eddie's yacht by the VHF radio and got through right away. The captain answered the radio call and asked Alan to hold while he got Eddie.

"Eddie here. Over."

"Eddie, Alan here. Over."

"Read you loud and clear. Over."

"I may need your help and want to see if you are available over the next month. Over."

"Roger that. Owner will not be back for two months, and we are in Fort Lauderdale docked at Pier Sixty-Six. Over."

"I'll be on a plane tomorrow. I'll meet you at the yacht tomorrow afternoon. Over."

"Roger that. See you tomorrow. Over and out."

Alan flew in and was at the yacht the next afternoon. Eddie was waiting for him on deck when he arrived.

"Eddie, let's take a walk."

They took a walk to the end of the dock, which had empty slips. Alan explained the situation and the contract offer in detail. Eddie just kept smiling the whole time. When Alan finished, Eddie kept smiling and immediately said, "Piece of cake."

Alan could not stop laughing; he leaned over and hugged Eddie.

"You saved my ass from that RPG in 'Nam, and you paid for it. Lucky you had your own personal fine-ass nurse to fix you up. You don't have to pay me anything. I'll gladly do this for free."

"No, buddy, you are going to get paid; I'll negotiate your contract. You can take your hostess on the yacht to Europe," Alan said with a chuckle.

"OK. I'll let my captain know I'm taking a break and will pack up and be ready to fly out tomorrow. Do you want me to fly directly to Providenciales in the Turks and Caicos?"

"Yes. The vessel is *Big Time*. She's a Palmer Johnson one-hundred-twenty-eight-footer. Make sure you get her set to sail ASAP. We are going to have a vendor do all the cleaning and prepare the cabins."

"Roger that. See you soon," Eddie said as they walked back to his yacht. They hugged and then bumped fists, drew their open hands back like an explosion, and crisply saluted.

Alan went directly back to the airport in Ft. Lauderdale to catch a flight to Dulles. He landed in the early evening, and the car was waiting to take him directly to CIA headquarters. He went directly to Robert's office. Robert's secretary had already left. Alan walked in and stuck his head in Robert's office door. "Can I come in?"

"Sure. I've been waiting for you. Come on in."

"Eddie is on his way to the yacht in the morning to get the vessel ready to sail. He agreed to a contract of fifteen thousand dollars for the completion of the mission."

"Wow, he has a good agent," Robert said with a chuckle. "Works for me. I'll have it written up tomorrow with the nondisclosure agreement and top-secret requirement. You can bring it to him to sign and then send it back to me. Rene is flying to Providenciales tomorrow afternoon. Natalie caught a red-eye to Miami and will be there tomorrow as well. The rest of the team is already on the yacht. I have the identity and document guys waiting for you. I'll wait for you and buy you dinner. You are booked to fly out tomorrow, connecting through Miami, and we have a charter flight set to get you to Providenciales in the early evening."

Alan went down the stairs to the identity and document unit, where they had everything ready and waiting. They dyed his hair and beard blond. They provided a color brush for his beard to take care of new growth. Finally they gave him contacts that made his eyes blue. Alan slipped them in, and they were ready to take his passport photo. Alan looked in the mirror while they worked on the passport and was surprised by how different he looked with these changes. "Wow, guys. Good job. I had to take a second look at myself," he said, smiling.

They finished the passport, and it was perfect. They gave him a packet that included a current USCG captain's license and a bio of his background and experience as a charter captain.

Alan met Robert, and they went to dinner. Afterward, Robert dropped Alan off at the Radisson in Langley.

The next morning Alan was picked up by a car, and the commercial flight down to Miami was right on time. The first officer of the chartered Learjet was waiting for him at the gate, and a car was waiting on the tarmac to take them to the private aircraft area of the airport. The chartered flight down was smooth and right on schedule. Alan caught a cab to the marina where the *Big Time* was docked. She was a real beauty and a classic world-class yacht. She was lit up and shining like a jewel. Alan walked up the gangway and carried his duffel into the main cabin. He could hear people working all over the boat. He heard someone coming down the stairwell and walked over to the bottom. Eddie came around the bulkhead and down the last set of stairs.

"Look at you, blond hair and blue eyes; you look like a surfer dude. This vessel is one awesome baby. Talk about the best money could buy. One of the other team members said this was a drug seizure, and that certainly makes sense. This baby cost a bundle. Oh, by the way, I met Natalie..." Eddie said with a big grin on his face.

Alan could not help but smile, and that got a big laugh out of Eddie. "I knew it."

"I got you fifteen thousand dollars for your contract."

"Fifteen thousand US dollars?"

"Yes, but of course as your agent, I'll keep ten percent," Alan replied with a big laugh.

"Damn, brother. That's awesome. Thanks."

"Round everyone up, and let's have a preliminary meeting in the main saloon. Where is my cabin?"

"Captain's cabin looks like the owner's stateroom on a normal yacht. Follow me," Eddie said. He led Alan to his cabin directly behind the bridge.

Alan noted the captain's whites hanging in the open closet. His everyday uniform—khaki shorts and a dark blue polo shirt with the vessel logo and name and four stripes on each shoulder—was laid out on the bed. Alan quickly changed and headed down to the main saloon.

When Alan entered the main saloon, everyone was there. He could not help but do a double take at Natalie. She had on her crew shorts and polo shirt, with her hair in a ponytail. She looked beyond amazing. Eddie was standing behind her and chuckled all the way to the dining room table. Alan walked over to the new team members, introduced himself, and shook hands.

"Well, guys, great to see everyone and meet the new team members. I'm ready to finish this and turn the last page of a bad chapter with these guys. Everyone sitting at this table is a top-notch field operator, and we also have a great chef," he said with a smile.

Everyone chuckled.

"Now let's get down to the assignment," Alan continued. "First, we have to make sure this yacht is impeccably ready for this charter; we need to be ready and have total credibility when they arrive. We will go out several times over the next week and a half to make sure everyone is sharp and professional. You all got the four action options of how we finish this ops assignment. It was sent to you on burn paper. I'll need each person to confirm the documents have been burned the day before the syndicate guys are scheduled to arrive. We don't know if they are going to have a team inspect the vessel, but I would expect they will. All our weapons are stored in a freshwater tank in waterproof bags. They are only accessible from the engine room and require removal of ten nuts on a bolted steel hatch. Any questions yet?"

They all just shook their heads no.

"There will be a total of ten guests. They are all males and all extremely dangerous. You all received information on each guy, again on burn paper; this must be burned the day before they arrive. I know four of you speak Spanish, but I want everyone but Rene to state they don't speak Spanish. This will hopefully allow us to pick up undercurrent issues that they don't want us to know. Our command order is the following: I'm in command of the mission, Rene is second in command, and Natalie is third in command. Almost all of us usually work alone, but this is team time. Finally, we will have a radio system with microphones and earpieces for each crew person to assure great service on the vessel. Nothing related to the mission is to ever be mentioned or discussed on this system. Any questions?"

Again everyone shook his or her head no.

"The emergency radio call is 'tiger shark.' The code for mission choice will use the same numbering system as designated in your mission packet. The mission call will be as follows: 'We have a number one, two, three, or four. Go.' The trigger code will be a radio announcement, 'Engineer to the bridge.' The timing parameters for each option start at that time. Stay flexible, and adjust to circumstances. Every one of these guys is a ruthless killer; stay alert one hundred percent of the time. Any questions? The floor is open."

Natalie held up her hand, and Alan motioned for her to proceed. "What if one of these losers tries to make an aggressive move with one of us ladies?"

"Great question. I know every woman sitting at this table could do serious damage or kill someone. The rules are to stop the physical advance verbally and then call me on the radio, stating passenger issue and your location. Just stay defensive to protect yourself. We will have backup to you posthaste."

"OK, from this point on, only alias names to be used. Let's do this," Alan finished. Everyone got up and moved out.

Natalie waited patiently until everyone had left and then walked over to Alan. "Hello, mate. I was surprised and pleased when I got the call for this one. Good to see you again."

"Good to see you as well, mate. I certainly have my key A-team members. FYI, Rene and I go back to 'Nam Operation Phoenix. That's why he is the number-two person."

"No problem. I am flattered to be in the number-three position. How have you been since Bordeaux?"

"Doing OK. Really want this to end."

"Don't worry, mate; Eddie told me this will be a piece of cake. Quite a character, he is. He guessed you and me immediately—ten minutes after he met me. I am not exactly sure how to interpret that with you Yanks, but I like him a lot."

"Eddie and I were marine recon together in 'Nam; he was my sniper. He is famous for 'piece of cake.' I'll have to tell you the story after this is over and I buy you a pint with Eddie."

"OK, mate. Let's get this done," she said. She hugged him and kissed him on the cheek. Alan could not take his eyes off of her as she walked out the room.

The rest of the time before the guests' arrival, the crew drilled and sailed twice. They were a well-oiled machine running the vessel, and the chef and hostesses served gourmet dinners every night to practice that important part of the charter operation. The meals were all outstanding. All reports were burned. Locked and loaded.

CHAPTER 25

SHOWTIME

The syndicate group was scheduled to arrive at 11:30 a.m., and the crew did a final wash down of the yacht. It was ready for the charter guests. All the crew had changed into their dress whites, and they were ready to greet the guests. Three SUVs arrived at 11:45 a.m., and the drivers opened the rear compartments and removed their bags, placing them at the bottom of the gangway. The charter guests climbed the gangway and were directed back to the stern deck, where the entire crew was lined up. Once all the guests were on the aft deck, Alan stepped forward.

"I am Captain Lance Daniels. Welcome to the yacht *Big Time.* We are here to make sure you will remember this charter trip for the rest of your lives. You will note all crew have name badges for your convenience. We have champagne and small-plate food waiting for you in the main saloon. Formal lunch will be served once we are underway. We will get your bags to your assigned cabins." Alan swept his hand toward Natalie. "Martha here is your steward and will make sure we take care of your needs on board the vessel. Welcome aboard," Alan finished as Natalie directed the guests to the grand saloon.

One of the men walked over to Alan. "Captain, I am in charge of security for our group while we travel. I will need to do an inspection of the vessel. Can you assign one of your crew to attend with me?"

"No problem; I'll have our first mate assist you," Alan quickly responded. He called Eddie over. "This is my first mate, James. James, can you please show their security man around the vessel?"

"Will do, Captain," Eddie said as he led the security man into the vessel.

The rest of the guests were enjoying the champagne and food and within a half hour were laughing and having a good time. The yacht was ready to depart, and the lines were let go. Alan skillfully maneuvered the vessel away from the dock, swung the bow toward the channel, and steered the vessel toward the sea buoy.

After Alan had passed the sea buoy and gotten up to cruising speed, Eddie called on the radio, "The security man has finished the rest of the vessel and would like to visit the bridge. Over."

"Bring him up. Over."

Eddie and the security man entered the bridge. Alan asked Eddie to take the helm and advised him the autopilot was set.

"Well, sir, is everything to your liking and approval?" Alan asked the security man.

"Yes. James was very helpful. My name is Ruiz. I just wanted to see the bridge and run through some final items with you. We will be having some highly confidential meetings, and we will be using the main saloon dining area. We do not want any crew in that area while we are meeting. If we need anything, we will send someone out. We do want the meeting area set up for drinks and food."

"Let me call up the steward now. Stand by. Martha, can you please come to the bridge? Over."

"I am on the way, Captain. Over."

In five minutes Natalie arrived.

"Martha, this is Mr. Ruiz," Alan said. "He is in charge of security and is organizing the confidential meetings the guests will be having while on board. Please sit down with Mr. Ruiz and make sure we provide for their meeting needs."

"Thank you, Captain," Mr. Ruiz said. "I have one last question for you. How many of your crew members speak Spanish?"

"Only one crew member, our second mate, speaks Spanish. I can introduce him to you. I am sorry we don't have more people who speak Spanish."

"All of us speak English, so there will not be a problem."

Ruiz left with Natalie.

Alan walked over to Eddie at the helm. Eddie gave him a thumbs-up and smiled; nothing else needed to be said.

The first planned anchorage was French Cay, which was two hours away at ten knots. *Big Time* was anchored, and the guests began their meetings that afternoon. Dinner went smoothly, and the guests loosened up much more after dinner while drinking on the aft deck area. Alan took the first anchor watch, with Eddie set to relieve him at 8:00 p.m.

When Alan came off watch, he headed for the crew galley to eat. Natalie was already there grabbing a quick bite before heading back up to oversee service for the guests. "Well, I have already been offered a very large sum of money to join one of the guests in his cabin tonight," Natalie said when Alan walked in.

"I don't blame him," Alan said with a smile.

"Very funny, mate. Got to get back," she said. She hugged and kissed Alan and swatted him on the ass on the way out.

Alan ate the prepared food for the crew and made a radio announcement that they would be picking up anchor and underway tomorrow on schedule. Then he went to his cabin. *This is going very well, and they are relaxing quicker than planned. Day six off North Caicos is looking perfect.*

The next four days went very well. They moved to different islands every day. Each day the guests held their meetings after breakfast, only stopping to eat lunch. They would finish up before dinner and then would relax and drink the rest of the night. On this fifth day, after the meeting, it was apparent that three of the men had been anointed as part of the syndicate leadership. The groupings after dinner showed a clear pattern of the men who had been chosen.

Alan was in his cabin when he received a radio call from Natalie advising him Ruiz wanted to meet with him. Alan told Natalie to bring him up to the bridge. Alan was waiting when they arrived.

"Captain, we have concluded our meetings, and these last two days before returning to Providenciales are recreational. Tomorrow where will we be?"

"Tomorrow we will be at Grand Turk. Excellent beaches. Sport-fishing trips can be set up, and there is world-class diving."

"Great. We want you to anchor near the best beach, and we want to go ashore. We want a catered lunch and drinks while we are on the beach. In the afternoon, six of us want to go sport fishing if you can arrange it."

"We will take care of everything. We will be anchored at nine in the morning and can take you and your guests to the beach any time after that. We will launch both nineteen-foot Boston Whalers to set up catering and bring your guests to the beach. I'll get on the radio now and set up the sport fishing."

"Well, Captain, keep up this level of service and make the last three days work out, and you and your crew are going to get a very big tip."

"Thank you, Mr. Ruiz; we aim to please," Alan replied. Natalie smiled and led Ruiz back down below.

Alan made the call on the marine radio to the Langley number. The man who answered posed as the representative of his charter office and Alan requested the sport-fishing trip for tomorrow afternoon with a local vendor. He also advised that day six would be North Caicos and he was concerned the "engineer was not feeling well" and they might need a replacement. The engineer would decide at North Caicos if he could remain.

The next morning at crew breakfast, Alan was eating with Eddie, Rene, and Natalie. "Looks like the night of day six at North Caicos will be the right time and place. I have decided to do option three. Any thoughts or comments?"

They all sat quietly for a minute before Eddie spoke first: "Piece of cake." This evoked a big laugh from every one.

"Sounds good to me," Rene replied.

"Same here, mate," Natalie agreed.

"OK. I'll make the radio announcement tomorrow night for the crew. Rene, why don't you go down and chat with the engineer?"

"Roger that," he replied before they all got up to leave.

The charter trip continued to move smoothly at Grand Turk. Natalie did an excellent job on the beach setup and catering. The afternoon sport fishing was on a forty-two-foot Bertram sub chartered from a local company; fishing was exceptional, and several trophy fish were caught. The six men who went sport fishing were the top leaders with their newly added partners.

After the beach outing was wrapped up, everyone was back on *Big Time* for early-evening cocktails before dinner.

Ruiz spotted Alan on his way up to the bridge. "Captain, today was superb. Not only are you and your crew going to get a very large tip, but we have already decided to make this an annual event."

"I'm so glad to hear you and your guests are enjoying the cruise and service. Our goal is to make sure you remember this charter for the rest of your lives," Alan replied before continuing on to the bridge.

The next morning they prepared the vessel and hoisted the two Boston Whalers back on board with the electric davits. Then they picked up anchor and were underway at 7:00 a.m., on course for North Caicos. The charter guests relaxed and drank all day. The guests were now becoming more aggressive with the female staff; Natalie only smiled and thanked them for their offers before saying no for the fourth time.

Big Time arrived at North Caicos at 1:00 p.m. and dropped anchor. The crew was serving lunch to the charter guests when Alan came in after confirming the anchor was set.

"Welcome to North Caicos, our last island stop before we return you to Providenciales. The island has miles of pure white-sand beaches and the largest flock of pink flamingos in the island chain. We will be launching the Boston Whalers, and they will be at your disposal."

"Captain, can we take the Boston Whalers ourselves?" Ruiz asked.

"Do you have persons with proper experience operating a vessel of this type?"

"Yes, we do."

"Yes, but you will all have to sign an additional waiver of liability."

"No problem, Captain. Get it ready for us to sign after lunch."

After lunch Alan set up for all the guests to sign. "Can we take some of the hostesses with us for catering and serving?" Ruiz said after signing.

"Not without at least one of my male crew. Company rules."

"Never mind; they can pack us lunch and drinks."

The charter guests spent the rest of the day out on the island; the six top guys were in one boat, and the other four were in the other boat. When they came back, they were very much intoxicated, and they all went to their cabins to shower and change for dinner.

Alan made an announcement to the crew over the radio system. "Last night. We have an option three go for shift watches. I repeat, option three go."

Dinner went well, and the charter guests had now been drinking for eight hours. Natalie and the two hostesses, all in their dress whites, came out with trays of shot glasses. "Gentlemen, on your final night, the crew toasts you. Kamikaze shots."

There was a big round of applause from the charter guests, and they began drinking. At midnight the last of the guests, the top six guys, were finishing their cognacs. By 12:30 a.m. all the guests were in their cabins. Rene, Natalie, and Eddie all came to the bridge, where Alan was standing anchor watch.

"Well, Ruiz's final offer tonight was one hundred thousand dollars," Natalie said with a chuckle.

"Everyone is ready; the dive tanks have been loaded on the Boston Whalers. Just give us the trigger code, and it will be like clockwork," Rene said.

They went below to wait.

At 1:30 a.m., Alan made the trigger code call from the bridge: "Engineer to the bridge. Over."

Alan walked onto the bridge wing, and within ten minutes, he could see small amounts of dark black smoke beginning to come out of the stack vents. The emergency alarm began to sound its regular blasts, and the emergency lights were all flashing. The charter guests, still drunk and now half-asleep, came staggering out of the cabins and were ushered to the emergency station on the stern deck. Heavy black smoke was now pouring out of the stack vents. The alarms and flashing lights caused sensory overload for the drunk, half-awake men waiting with Natalie and Eddie on the stern deck.

Alan jogged out to the aft deck. "Gentlemen, we have a major fire in the engine room; the automatic fire suppression system did not extinguish the fire. We have three crewmen in fire suits with oxygen tanks fighting the fire by hand. We have a large storage of propane on the vessel, and for safety purposes, I'll need you all to get in the Boston Whalers and move one hundred meters away to the starboard side of the vessel. I need every crewman here. Can you and your men handle the Whalers?" he asked, holding a hand-held radio out to Ruiz.

"Of course, Captain; we will move away on the boats and await your call to us with the all-clear," Ruiz replied.

The men loaded into the boats and started the motors. Eddie untied their bowlines, and they began moving off to the starboard side of the vessel. Alan moved back in, and the engineer shut off all lights on the vessel except for the emergency lights. Rene was just coming into the main saloon.

"Are the timers set for twenty minutes?" Alan asked.

"Yes; activated them as soon as they were fifty meters from the stern. We are eleven minutes and counting," Rene replied as they both headed for the bridge.

Alan pulled out his infrared scope, which had a range indicator function, and checked the distances of the Boston Whalers. They were slightly over 110 meters away. Perfect.

"They are the right distance."

Black smoke was still pouring out of the stack vents of *Big Time*, and the emergency signal was blaring, with only emergency lights on in the vessel.

Natalie came to the bridge with Alan and Rene. Suddenly there was a flash and the sound of an explosion, followed seconds later by another flash and explosion where the Boston Whalers had been drifting. Eddie and one of the deckhands had already pushed off in the inflatable, heading over to where the Boston Whalers had been. They were gone for an hour.

"Well done. I think the last-minute addition of the kamikazes sealed the deal."

"Perfect! Those were some completely lost puppies," Rene said with a chuckle.

The lights came back on, and the emergency alarm was turned off. The black smoke stopped pouring out of the stack vents.

"We have been one hundred percent effective," Eddie finally radioed in. "Found all ten; weights were attached. We are on our way back. Over."

"All hands to the main saloon," Alan radioed out to the crew.

Eddie and the deckhand were the last in to the main salon.

"Well, I must say everyone did an outstanding job," Alan said. "I want Natalie to organize a search of their cabins in the morning. We will be underway tomorrow at zero eight hundred for our scheduled rendezvous. I want the life-raft debris canister discharged over the side as well as some random clothing from the guests. Also prepare the emergency beacon. Get some rest," Alan said, closing the post-action brief.

Natalie held up her hand.

"Yes, Natalie?"

"We have two kamikazes for everyone to take the edge off—the new A-team drink of choice," she said as she walked over to the bar with one of the hostesses.

Everyone laughed, and several gave a "Hear, hear."

The trays were brought back, and everyone took the first shot. Natalie called out, "Cheers!"

The second one went down even quicker, and then they were off to their cabins.

Alan had been back in his cabin for ten minutes when there was a knock. He opened the door, and Natalie was standing with a sexy smile. Alan laughed and pulled her in the cabin. Great finish to the assignment.

The next morning they discharged the canister with vessel debris and threw all the life rings and ten life jackets with the vessel name overboard. They also threw some clothing from the charter guests overboard, as well as some crew uniforms. Finally, they threw *Big Time*'s emergency beacon overboard. The Langley technical unit had set the emergency beacon to go live five hours after it was deployed to broadcast a constant emergency signal for aid.

The debris from the two Boston Whalers was also floating nearby. They picked up anchor and were underway, heading east in the Atlantic.

Twenty-five miles offshore, Alan picked up the radar image at the exact planned position. Eddie took the binoculars and picked up the conning tower as the submarine started to surface. The attack sub began to open its hatches as it approached. Alan maneuvered to fifty yards away. Seas were a light swell out of the southeast, and both vessels laid bow to the swell. Rene and Eddie launched the inflatable and motored over to the sub. Then they ferried the five men who had come on the submarine's deck to the yacht. The first thing the new crew did was to remove the film-applied name *Big Time* from the stern of the vessel and apply the new name, *Sundowner,* in its place.

Alan's crew had packed up, and they began transferring back to the submarine. Within an hour and a half, Alan's crew had transferred to the submarine, and the new crew for *Sundowner* was ready to get underway—destination Monte Carlo.

The captain of the attack submarine was waiting for Alan and his team in the wardroom. "Welcome on board *Bluefin.* Your ETA Puerto Rico Roosevelt Roads Naval Base is two days. If this is your first time on a submarine, space is tight. You will be sleeping two to a cabin, and five of you will be in the multibunk crew area. Mr. Joubert will decide the sleeping arrangements. Mr. Joubert, I need you in the con, as Langley is awaiting your call."

Alan advised Rene to decide sleeping arrangements and headed to the con with the captain. The captain handed Alan a satellite telephone and brought him up to the deck on top of the conning tower. "I'll leave you here, Mr. Joubert. Come down when you're finished, and we will be submerging," he said as he headed down the ladder.

"Robert, we're done. It went like clockwork."

"Excellent. Your first submarine ride?"

"Yep, sure is. The team you gave me was incredible. It couldn't have gone smoother."

"Call me when you get back and settled," Robert said before signing off.

Alan climbed down the ladder, and a crewman went up after him and closed the hatch. Then the dive alarm went off.

"Mr. Joubert, would you and some of your team like a tour?" the captain asked.

"Thanks, but later, if we can, Captain? We had a late night yesterday, and I know we all just want to get some rest."

Alan was led to a cabin and opened the door to find Natalie sitting on the lower bunk, smiling. "Well, mate, you are about to be a member of the five-hundred-feet-deep club," she said as she stood up and wrapped her arms around Alan's neck. She kissed him deeply and kicked the cabin door closed.

CHAPTER 26

GOOD TO BE HOME

The trip back to Roosevelt Roads Naval Base on the *Bluefin* was uneventful. The team received tours of the sub, and Alan was allowed to steer the sub for a short time and change dive depth.

They arrived on schedule, and two vans were waiting to drive them back to San Juan. Both vans first went to the Muñoz Rivera Airport in San Juan to drop off all the crew except for Natalie, Rene, and Eddie.

Alan got out of the van while the team members unloaded their gear. He shook hands and thanked all of the team members before they departed. The van dropped Natalie and Alan off at his condo and took Rene and Eddie to the La Concha Hotel two blocks away.

Rene and Eddie came over an hour and a half later; they all went bodysurfing at the beach at Alan's condo. Natalie looked magnificent in her bikini. Alan barbequed steaks, and they finished off the last of Alan's Saint-Émilion bottles. Rene and Eddie were scheduled to fly out the next morning.

"Well, guys, I can't thank you enough for removing this sword that has been hanging over my head. Especially you, Eddie—our first-class hired mercenary," Alan said with a big laugh. He stood up and gave the famous Puerto Rican toast, "Good luck in health, love, and money, and time for it all," as they all clicked their glasses.

The next morning Alan and Natalie gave Rene and Eddie a ride to the airport and walked them to their gate for their flight to Miami. Alan gave them each a hug. Then each bumped fists, pulling their hands back open like an explosion, and then crisply saluted. Natalie hugged them both, and they boarded the aircraft.

Alan and Natalie drove back to the condo, and Alan called Robert.

"Robert here."

"The team members, except for Natalie, have all flown out. What is the chatter?"

"Everything is looking good. The beacon went off as planned with your emergency radio recordings. There was a merchant ship nearby, and it proceeded to the site and reported only debris and no survivors. The crew recovered one of the life rings with the vessel name. A coast guard officer called the emergency contact number for the charter guests. He advised the vessel had reported a fire and the subsequent explosion was probably caused by the vessel's propane tank; and they had only found a debris field. No survivors, either guests or crew. Chatter in Venezuela is sorrow and disbelief—no signs of any suspicion. We will carefully monitor our wiretaps for at least a month more to assure this has been put to rest."

"I feel like a five-hundred-pound weight has been lifted from my shoulders. FYI, we used option three. We had some good luck, and the syndicate guys asked to operate the Boston Whalers the day before. That made things much less complicated; no crew had to go out with them for the abandon-ship alert. Those antiperson-nel mines in the dive tanks were extremely effective; timers made to look like regulators worked perfectly. Tell the backroom plan-ning guys I owe them a dinner."

"How long is Natalie staying?"

"She is going to stay a week and take time off. I'll be taking the week off as well unless you have a code red."

"Roger that. Enjoy, Alan. You are a lucky dog and always have been," Robert said before signing off.

Alan and Natalie spent the next three days enjoying the beach life, salsa dancing, barbequing, and drinking beers and margaritas. They ran every day in Luchetti Park and bodysurfed. Alan was truly enjoying both his time with her and the freedom of not having to worry about his work with the Absolute Resolution. Natalie was a beautiful, sexy woman and a real joy to spend time with. The sex was world class, athletic with an edge.

The morning before Natalie was scheduled to fly out, Alan again fixed his favorite Manhattan omelet.

When they finished, Natalie spoke first. "Well, mate, I certainly have enjoyed my time with you again. I hope we can see each other again in the future."

"You can bet on that, mate. I want you to know I lost my fiancée last year, and I'm still struggling with those feelings."

"Robert told me about it. I understand you took care of the people responsible."

"Not officially," he replied.

"Understood."

"Today I am going to take you to the famous bikini store in Condado and buy you a few; they are my present to you—and of course me as well."

Alan bought her five bikinis, and she modeled each one.

"OK, mate. No more." She laughed.

Alan paid, and they went to lunch. When they got back to the condo they went bodysurfing. Alan rented chairs and an umbrella on the beach and they spent the rest of the afternoon relaxing and drinking a couple of beers. Natalie told Alan her story of growing up privileged in East Sussex and then letting her parents know she wanted to join the Special Air Service. Alan provided a brief on

'Nam, Eddie, and their time together. Natalie burst out laughing when Alan told the history of Eddie and "piece of cake."

After the beach, they went for a run. Natalie ran stride for stride with Alan on the three-mile run. Walking back to the condo, they discussed plans for the night.

"Your last night, mate. I'm planning dinner at the Metropol and then salsa dancing. Does that work for you?" Alan asked.

"Sounds marvelous. Let's do it."

They showered and dressed, with Natalie using the extra bedroom to get ready. When she walked out, Alan was speechless. She was wearing a strapless, straight blue dress and high-heeled shoes. The dress was the exact same color as her eyes. She was perfectly tanned, and her curly brown hair was loose on her shoulders. Alan's hair was still blond, but he had shaved his beard. He was dressed in a white linen guayabera shirt and dark-blue cotton pants.

"Natalie, you look absolutely stunning," Alan said. He walked over to hold her hands and turn her around. "Simply stunning."

"Not bad yourself, mate."

They took a cab to the Metropol. Dinner was excellent, and every man in the restaurant watched Natalie's every move when she walked into the dining room. They finished dinner and caught a cab over to La Concha. Natalie was a very talented dancer and had picked up salsa like a natural, adding her own extra flair. Alan had a scotch, and Natalie had a martini. They danced for an hour before Natalie finally gave Alan the "let's go" look and hand sign. Alan settled the bill, and they walked out to the lobby.

"I have to take these shoes off for the walk back," she said. She put her hand on Alan's shoulder and pulled off one shoe and then the other. They started to walk back to the condo; Natalie was barefoot carrying her shoes and Alan had his arm wrapped around her shoulder.

They were halfway back to the condo when they heard a girl screaming from a driveway between two buildings. "Let me go.

Leave me alone," she screamed. Natalie dropped her shoes, and they both started to jog into the alley. They could see a woman and two men twenty yards ahead.

"Leave her alone," Alan commanded in Spanish.

"Get out of here. This is none of your business," one of the men replied in Spanish.

When Alan and Natalie reached the men, the woman was standing with her back against the wall with the two men standing in front of her.

"Leave her alone. She wants you to leave her alone," Alan commanded. Natalie stepped over to the side of the two men.

At that moment, the two men turned, with drawn pistols pointed at Alan. "Go back to the hotel, and let them know we have him," one of the men said to the woman, who laughed and pushed by Alan on her way out of the alley.

"Mr. Joubert, please put your hands on your head. Young lady, step to the side, and don't say or do anything, and you will not be hurt. Good to finally meet you, Mr. Joubert. We spoke on the telephone once before you cheated Cuba out of a quarter of a million dollars for the oil and oil barge."

"Captain Rodriguez. Yes, I do remember. What a surprise to see you in Puerto Rico."

"My Russian friend and I are here to solve a constant and ongoing problem for both of us, and that is you, Mr. Joubert. Young lady, we will not hurt you; remain quiet, and do not move. We will bind your hands and feet, and you will be found in the morning."

The Russian came over to Alan and patted him down. "Clean. No weapon."

"OK, Mr. Joubert, hold your hands out in front of you," Rodriguez said as he walked over with a zip tie. Alan could see Natalie was setting her position; they were not paying any attention to her. Both gunmen had lowered their guns, and now Natalie had moved slightly behind the left shoulder of the Russian.

Rodriguez holstered his pistol and started to put the zip tie on Alan's wrists. At that moment Natalie pivoted and completed a perfect head kick on the Russian, launching him against the wall. He dropped his gun. Alan immediately lifted his knee as high as he could into Rodriguez's groin. Rodriguez bent in half, holding his groin, and Alan struck him with his right elbow, driving it hard across his jaw. Rodriguez crumpled to the ground. Natalie had already picked up the Russian's pistol; he lay lifeless against the wall. Alan pulled Rodriguez's pistol and found his zip ties. He and Natalie hog-tied the men with zip ties.

"Let's get back home so I can call Robert," Alan said, and they took off running. As soon as they got to the condo, he opened his safe and pulled out a Berretta for himself and one for Natalie.

He then quickly called Robert.

"Robert here."

"Natalie and I just got ambushed by a Cuban and a Russian. I am only talking to you because they had no idea who Natalie was. We have them zip-tied in the alley three buildings away but need to get someone there quick, as they were working with a team that had a woman and undetermined more. I expect they are staying in a hotel close by. The Cuban was Captain Rodriguez, the guy I dealt with on the telephone for the oil barge in Cuba."

"The one the vessel owner shortchanged a quarter of a million?"

"Yes, but it was about much more than that. He mentioned I had been an ongoing problem for both the Cubans and the Russians. Can you get the FBI SWAT guys to pick these guys up ASAP? We need to get these guys interrogated."

"Will do. You two stay tight. I'll get back to you shortly."

They waited on full alert. Alan, with Natalie's help, moved the dining room table, laying it on its side with the top against the door.

"Well, mate, sure glad you were here tonight. They had no idea who you were. I must say, that was one outstanding move on the Russian," Alan said with awe.

"Well, the Cuban is certainly wishing he had not finally met you. Left my favorite shoes back there," she said with a chuckle.

The telephone rang. "Alan, the FBI SWAT guys scrambled right away, and still those two got away," Robert said. "The woman must have come back because they were taking so long, and that certainly would indicate they are staying close. We have the police and the FBI starting a search of the hotels for them. We are also doing a search of incoming flights. You two stay put. Thank heavens Natalie was with you. I'll need you both to fly up tomorrow. You have two FBI SWAT guys with automatic rifles in a vehicle outside your condo. I'll get back to you on the security to get you both to the airport." Robert signed off.

Natalie walked over and hugged and kissed Alan. "You are done here in Puerto Rico, mate. You are compromised, and the horses are out of the barn."

Alan walked over to the sofa and sat down with his head in his hands. He of course had realized this in the alley, but Natalie saying it confirmed what he knew in his heart was true.

Natalie walked over and held Alan's face in her hands. "It's going to be OK, mate. This is the nature of our work. You have had a great long run. I know how tough this is, but you will move on, and you can do all alias assignments like me."

"I'll really miss my Sea Secure family and the work. The top guy, George, was my mentor. The staff in San Juan was like family. I love the marine-consulting work."

"I know, Alan, but the Cubans and Russians are after you now, and they know your name and where you live. It is not *if* they will get you; it is when. Robert will tell you the same thing tomorrow."

The telephone rang, and it was Robert. "The FBI SWAT team guys are taking you to the air base at Roosevelt Roads, departing your condo at zero seven hundred. They will pick you up in the garage, which will be secured. We have a Learjet there that will bring you both to Miami, where you will catch an Eastern Airlines flight to Dulles. A car will pick you up and bring you here. See you in the afternoon."

"What about my personal items at the office and all my clothes and furniture at my condo? What about my staff? Alan asked with concern.

"Don't worry. George will handle your staff. You will be leaving unexpectedly to pursue other interests. You can call your staff when you get to Miami. Keep why you are leaving only that- pursuing other interests. Your secretary will pack up your personal items at work and mail them to an CIA cover address in New Orleans. The CIA will arrange to pack everything at your condo and ship it to storage in Miami for now. Bring your pistols and all your ops gear with you," Robert said quietly.

"Roger that," Alan replied with concern and sadness.

CHAPTER 27

DÉJÀ VU

The next morning the two FBI SWAT team members, fully equipped, picked Alan and Natalie up in the condo garage. Alan was quiet on the drive to the air station at Roosevelt Roads, and Natalie sat close to him with her head on his shoulder. The Learjet was waiting on the tarmac, and the FBI SUV dropped them off. They were the only passengers, and they were wheels up in twenty minutes.

"Listen, mate," Natalie said. "Everything is going to work out. I know they will take care of you. If you get some time off, come across the pond and visit. We could always go back to the Grand Hotel in Bordeaux."

"It will be very interesting to see what the powers that be have decided. I'll make sure they let you know. If I get time off, you can bet I'll be over to visit."

The Lear landed at Miami International Airport, and a car was waiting to take them across the tarmac to the commercial airline terminals. Natalie's flight on British Airways was departing an hour before Alan's flight, so he walked her to the gate.

"Take care of yourself, mate," Alan said quietly. "Again, thank you for saving my ass. Remind me not to get you mad. Safe trip back to London."

"You take care of yourself. Make sure Robert lets me know as soon as possible where I'll be able to reach you," Natalie replied before wrapping her arms around his neck and giving him a long kiss. "I will miss you a lot," she said as she turned to board the aircraft.

Alan's flight was on schedule to Dulles, and when he landed, the car was waiting to take him to Langley. Alan went directly to Robert's office, and Eileen told him to go right in. Robert was on a phone call and signaled for Alan to sit down.

When Robert hung up, they both stood up and shook hands. "How are you doing?" Robert asked.

"Still somewhat in shock that everything I have worked for is gone."

"Not everything."

"I really enjoyed the consulting work with Sea Secure, and the staff and especially George were a big part of my life. I also really enjoy Puerto Rico. Tell me you caught Rodriguez, the Russian, and the rest of their team."

"No, we didn't. By the time we found their hotel, they were gone. They just left everything behind. We had gone to full alert at the airport, but they have not shown up there. They are good. We are checking boat rentals and charter aircraft, but they seem to have just disappeared. The head FBI guy thinks they are lying low somewhere on the island waiting for things to cool down."

"That makes the most sense. OK, what is the word on me and my future?"

"I was talking to the top guy when you came in. He has asked me to give you two options. The first, the one we hope you take, is for you to move to the alias program, where all your work is completed using an alias rather than a deep cover. We will give you an everyday alias as well. This offer also includes giving you title to a Swan 47 sloop that you will run as a charter operation out of the Bahamas, just like the old days when I came back to get you. You will be on call for alias assignments for the Caribbean and Central and South America, the same as before." Robert paused.

"What is the second option?"

"You can walk away from the CIA. You will have a new alias, and we will help you get a new marine-consulting job in the US or Europe. Your service with the CIA would end, but we would pay you one hundred thousand a year for the next five years."

Alan sat quietly for several minutes. "I want to sleep on this one. Does George at Sea Secure know what is happening?"

"Yes. The top guy has already called him. When we are finished, you can give him a call."

"Great. I want to sleep on this and give George a call now. I'll see you in the morning."

"Eileen has your reservation at the Radisson; you can use my conference room to call George."

Alan called, and George's executive assistant asked him to hold.

George picked up. "Alan, I am so glad to hear from you."

"I understand you have been advised of my status."

"Yes. My ex-roomie called me yesterday. This is all about making sure you are safe. Don't worry at all about Sea Secure. We have lost an invaluable asset, but in the scheme of things, it doesn't compare to your safety."

"I am truly going to miss you, my staff, and my work with Sea Secure."

"I know, Alan; I completely understand and can only imagine how traumatic this must be for you. I understand from my ex-roomie you have a decision to make. I will be fully supportive and help you in any way I can regardless of your choice."

"Thanks, boss, and you will always be that: boss," Alan replied before they signed off.

Alan returned to the hotel, dropped off his bag, and caught the Metro to the Vietnam Memorial. He sat on a bench overlooking the awe-inspiring polished black-granite wall with more than fifty-eight thousand names etched in white. The title in the center said all that needed to be said: *All gave some, some gave all.* Alan sat quietly for two hours until the lights in the ground came on, illuminating the names with gold lighting. Then Alan returned to the hotel and immediately went to sleep.

The next morning Alan was waiting with Eileen when Robert came in the office. Robert walked him into his office and closed the door.

"Option one," Alan said.

"Talk about to the point. Excellent! The Swan 47 is docked at your old marina, Dinner Key in Coconut Grove. You can fly out today if you want."

"That would be great. What is the name of the boat?"

"The *Anne Bonny,* named after the famous woman pirate from Jamaica. She is at Pier B, slip forty-two. Keys are waiting with the harbormaster. We are going to give you two weeks off to get grounded. We're going to handle your advertising and all the booking. You just get to sail the boat and be ready to leave on an alias assignment when we need you."

"Thanks, Robert, and thank the top guy."

"You can do that yourself; I think he wants to touch your cape again," Robert replied with a chuckle. He stood up and then led Alan to the director's office.

The executive assistant of the director of the CIA brought them directly in when they arrived.

"Hello, Alan. So glad you're safe. That was a real close call."

"If Natalie had not been there, they would have had me. They were good."

"Well, I understand you are still on board. We have run out of awards to present you, but we are very happy you are staying on. Well done," he said. They shook hands, and then Alan left the office.

Alan flew down to Miami that afternoon. He was deep in thought for the entire flight. *I'll never be able to love anyone like I did Maria.* He knew this now after his time with both Liz and Natalie.

He also realized how close he had come to getting Liz in serious danger due to their relationship. It was not fair. *Natalie and I do have a common bond. We know the truth about our lives and the reality that each of our new assignments could be our last.*

Alan caught a cab to the Diner Cay Marina. When he arrived, it brought back a flood of memories of his life before Absolute Resolution. He slowly walked down to the harbor master's office, enjoying the sight of all of the many beautiful yachts and the sound of rigging lightly rattling in the breeze. The same harbor master was still running the marina. He handed Alan the keys. "Looks like you have made a real upgrade, my friend."

Alan walked down to the slip to see his new home. The Swan 47 was glistening white with a deep sea-blue stripe down the sides of the hull. She was an absolute beauty and a racehorse. He did a quick inspection, and she was fully equipped, including a roller-furling genoa, generator, and top-of-the-line electronics. The interior was all mahogany and was in perfect shape. The yacht was less than two years old.

Alan was just starting to unpack when his pager went off. He went to the pay telephone at the end of the dock and called Robert.

"Alan, I am pleased to advise you that you'll have your first charter tomorrow for two weeks to Great Exuma and then to Cat Island. I hope this is OK."

"I'm ready to jump back in. How many guests?"

"Just one," Robert replied. "Good first test run for your future business. The guest will be arriving tomorrow at eleven hundred hours." Robert signed off.

Well, here I am, back where I was when Robert came and got me off Cat Cay five years ago.

The next morning was a beautiful sunny day with a steady breeze. It was a perfect morning to set sail to the Bahamas. Alan sat in the cockpit with a cup of coffee, enjoying the peaceful beauty of the new day. He began to prepare the yacht for departure shortly after. He was on deck pulling off the mainsail cover when he saw her walking down the dock. He immediately jumped down and began running down the dock. Natalie dropped her bag and closed on Alan. He grabbed her, lifted her up, and swung her around. He then gave her a long kiss before he let her go.

"I volunteered to be your first test charter, mate, and I have very high standards," she said, wrapping her arms around his neck and giving him a long, deep kiss.

ABOUT THE AUTHOR

 Al Dugan was raised in New Orleans. After graduating from Jesuit High School, he received his degree from Louisiana State University.

Dugan spent thirty-six years in the Marine Insurance industry including twelve years as an intermediary for Lloyd's of London. Early in his career, Dugan received the Chairman's Award for outstanding service.

Dugan has extensive knowledge and experience in Puerto Rico and Central and South America.

Made in the USA
Middletown, DE
20 April 2017